# FREAKs

# FREAKs

---

## Joseph E. Scalia

josephescalia.com

Dedication

for my children
Janine, Ian, Jesse and Mikki
my own special freaks
for Carol Diamond who inspired this book
and for Leonora Goldberg, wherever you may be…

# Introduction

s a hot September morning somewhere around 1979. I was in Study Hall
feteria B at Hicksville Junior High School with about forty kids. None of
anted to be there because we all knew that Study Hall was a complete
e of time, and we could be doing something more productive. And I was
eacher! I was bemoaning my fate, counting the more productive things I
t be doing with my time, like finally getting around to writing the Great
rican Novel, a best seller that would allow me to quit my temporary
ing job and buy that Porsche 9-11 I had my eye on, or even straightening
ne sock drawer in my night table. When I looked up from my class book a
girl was standing in front of me waiting patiently. She was tiny and thin, a
al 7th Grader. Her dark hair was cut short like Buster Brown or the Dutch
on the paint cans. And she was crying.

"What's the problem?" I asked, though I knew it couldn't be anything
rtant compared to my own problems, and steeled myself for some
nificant matter that I'd have to address, like somebody throwing spitballs.

She lifted her glasses to wipe her eyes and there were little red dents
e sides of her nose. "I was late and I couldn't get my locker open and I don't
any books and now I'm going to be marked unprepared for my classes,"
aid in a rush. The tears were streaming down her face.

Even though I wasn't supposed to, I scribbled a pass on a scrap of
r and told her to go back to her locker and get the books she needed.

"Thank you," she said.

When she walked away I noticed that her right leg was turned in and
he walked with a limp, like a puppet with a twisted string. In that instant I
ed that this poor kid just starting junior high school was facing more
rtant things than not having her books or being late for Study Hall. She
d have to get through junior and senior

high school and put up with the taunts and the teasing and the insensitivities of her classmates for the next six years! It was an epiphany for me. I wanted to jump up and hug her and keep her safe and tell her that everything was going to be all right. But I didn't. I knew the truth. Instead, I decided then and there to write a short story and make that little girl with a limp the main character. And the idea for *FREAKs* was born. It took me three years to get the story, originally titled "Welcome To The Menagerie," on paper. And then it took another ten years of rewriting and revising, of testing the manuscript each year on my classes for their reactions and their input. In the process the idea grew from a short story into the novel *FREAKs*. And along the way the little girl who inspired my first novel grew up too. As Fate would have it, I lost contact with her after junior high and never had the opportunity to let her know the profound impact she had on me that morning in Study Hall, and how she has touched my life. Until now that is. Thank you, Carol. I hope your life has been a happy one.

Joseph E. Scalia 2004

Other books by the author:

*Pearl* (Xlibris ISBN 1-4010-0045-2 or 978-1-4010-0045-5)

*No Strings Attached* (Publish America ISBN 1-4137-0549-9 or 978-1-4137-0549-2)

*Brooklyn Family Scenes* (Tawny Girl Press ISBN 978-1-60402-882-9)

*Scalia vs. The Universe Or: My Life And Hard Times* (Tawny Girl Press

ISBN 978-1-6042-883-6)

# Chapter One
## "First Day"

My name is Hilda, but people call me Hildy. Hilda is a German name. My mother was German, and French a little. My father is American. I mean *real* American, from before Columbus. He's part Cherokee, and a whole lot of other stuff. I guess that makes me a mutt.

I used to go to Vanderville Junior High School on Long Island, in Nassau County. That was last year. Before that I went to schools in California, Michigan, Texas, and a couple of other places I can't even remember. I'm fifteen, almost, and already I've lived in more places than anybody I know. We travel a lot, Daddy and me.

My mother is dead. I guess my story really starts with her. She was a dancer. Not the ballroom type. She danced classical ballet. She committed suicide, I think, when I was just a little baby, so I don't remember her. We don't talk about it much, so I'm really not sure. Besides Daddy, my only other family is Grandma Olga and Grandpa Louis, my mother's parents. I lived with them for a few years when I was a baby, so we're pretty close. They used to have a big house in Connecticut, but now they're retired to Florida, so I don't see them too often.

Sometimes when Daddy looks at me, I know he's seeing my mother. He has a picture of her that he keeps in a silver frame. She was beautiful. Daddy says I look exactly like her. I don't really think so, but that's what he says. Maybe I do, in a way.

My father thinks I'm beautiful, but I've never regarded myself as even pretty. He calls me his "precious gem." He's a romantic and I guess I'm a realist.

Everything about me is average. My height, my weight. My brown hair is kind of mousy and I keep it cut short like a boy's. Less trouble that way. I wear glasses that leave little red dents on the sides of my nose when I read. And there are braces on my teeth. Two thousand dollars worth of orthodontia work that Daddy is still paying off in installments to Dr. Gresham in Van Nuys, California. Like I said, I'm really a realist.

My parents met while my mother was dancing with a small touring ballet company. Daddy said he fell in love the moment he saw her. Love at first sight, just like in the movies. And he followed her around the country until she agreed to marry him. It was all very romantic. It was a terrible shock for him when she died. That was soon after I was born. I'm still not exactly clear about what happened, and maybe I won't ever know for sure. But I guess it's like Daddy says, sometimes, bad things happen to good people.

After it happened Daddy started drinking and he lost his job. He left me with Grandma Olga for a while and took off somewhere, until he could "sort things out," he said. It took him a while, because I was four when he came back. There was a terrible fight with my grandparents when he announced that he was taking me with him.

For a while we just drifted from place to place, getting by a day at a time, but we had fun. I guess Daddy was still trying to forget, but he couldn't. That's the way it is, you know, you can't forget and you shouldn't forget the people you love. And that's only right.

I love the dance too. It's something I probably inherited from my mother. I used to dream about becoming a prima ballerina. Sometimes still, I just stand in front of the mirror studying myself in the various dance positions. Well, maybe not so much anymore. And I used to have this fantasy about dancing a command performance for the President of the United States or the Queen of England or somebody, to a standing audience.

I know it's silly and it's only a fantasy, and I'll never really do it. You see, I was born with a congenital hip defect and I had to wear a leg brace for a long time. I still walk with a limp.

I hate the word handicapped. My father says they handicap horses. And golfers have a handicap too. So anytime somebody says that I'm handicapped, I picture myself with a silly bunch of golfers dragging around a bunch of horses while we're trying to hit little white golf balls all over the place. It's good for a laugh.

I have to admit for a while I felt kind of responsible for my mother's death. After all, I was the imperfect product of two perfect people.

Once I tried to talk about it to Mrs. Pierce, the school psychologist in one of the schools I went to, but Daddy packed us up before I really got a chance, and we moved to another job in another part of the country. It's not that I feel guilty exactly, and Daddy doesn't blame me, I know. He still feels responsible himself. It's just that I can't help thinking how different things could have been in life if I was born normal, and if my mother was still alive.

Well, that's just some of the old stuff that I think about sometimes. And there's more, like everything that happened this past year in Vanderville. It's all still a jumble in my mind, and I haven't quite sorted things out. But I wonder why God, if there is a God, why He just sits around and allows some things to happen.

If I sound kind of like a philosopher, I guess it's because I am in a way. In all the hours that I've spent alone, I've had lots of time to think, and to read. More than most kids, I guess. And because of the way I was born, my life, so far, has certainly been different. I guess I am different from other girls my age, and not just because of my hip, I mean. It's not that I don't think about boys and nice clothes and makeup and stuff. It's just that the way things have turned out, those things aren't that important to me.

Anyway, it was the first day of school, my first day, I mean. The school year was pretty much well into the first semester when I got there. We had just moved to Long Island from Houston, Texas, and Daddy rented a little house for us in Nassau County. He had a new job with an electronics company that made parts for the Space Shuttle or something. Daddy's real smart, and he's had lots of jobs, so he can do almost anything. A jack-of-all-trades. Grandma Olga calls him "scattered." She says he doesn't apply himself, so he won't ever amount to much. But I don't think that's true, and I think she says it because she's still angry at him about the way things turned out.

I was sitting outside the Guidance Office of Vanderville Junior High School, holding the books that my father had picked up when he registered me for school the day before. I didn't particularly like the idea of being the "forever-new-girl" in school, but from all that moving around at least I had lots of experience and a lot of practice, so I wasn't nervous. Well, maybe just a little.

From what I had seen of Vanderville, it wasn't much different from the other places I'd been. It looked like a school. The sounds that I heard from my seat sounded like a school. It even smelled like a school. You know, a mixture of old tuna fish sandwiches, chalk dust and gym socks. The principal, a Mr. Fagan, was a nervous looking man, who seemed very busy when he rushed through the office. He didn't say anything to me, but he kind of smiled a little and ran out again.

I was waiting for Mr. Gentile, my new guidance counselor, who was out to lunch. When he arrived, I was doing dance exercises in my mind, in time with the music of the secretaries clicking out their work on computer keyboards. He was thin, thirty-five about, kind of cute and out of breath. He had nice eyes. It's the eyes that I usually notice first about people. Mr. Gentile had gentle eyes. But his fingers were stained yellow from smoking a lot, and I could smell tobacco on his clothes.

"I'm sorry I'm late," he said with a rush. "Er... Miss Crocket?" He looked at the index card he was holding. "Hilda. Why don't we go into my office? I have your schedule program made out, and a New Entrant slip for all your teachers to sign. Then I'll take you on a tour around the building. It's pretty big, but you'll get used to it. It won't be hard once you know where you're going."

I stood up and took a step towards him. Because of my hip problem my right foot points in and I move kind of on tiptoes. Someone once described the way I walk as a string puppet with a twisted string. I liked to think of it as a special way of dancing. But poor Mr. Gentile wasn't ready for it. I guess no one had warned him. The smile on his face vanished and the expression in his eyes changed to embarrassment and pity, just for a fraction of a second, until he recovered. I felt kind of sorry for him. He didn't know if he should help me, take my books, or just ignore it. So I just smiled.

We were out in the halls making the rounds of my classrooms. Mr. Gentile was right, it was a big building, but Vanderville wouldn't be too hard to negotiate. I had classes on every floor, and there were four of them. And I was scheduled for gym too. He apologized for that, and said he'd set up an alternate activities program so I could get course credit.

"Of course I'll find you an elevator key, and an early dismissal pass so you'll have plenty of time to get from class to class. I'll call Transportation at the Administration

Building to make arrangements for the special bus. And maybe I can juggle some room changes so you won't have to-"

"It's no bother, Mr. Gentile," I explained. "I actually prefer using the stairs. I'm really able to manage."

Then the bell rang and a stampede of kids shook the building. I pressed myself against the lockers and allowed the stream to rush past, but poor Mr. Gentile was caught in the flood. He tried to battle his way back to me like a fish fighting the current. That was when I saw them walking in front of me, three boys, who had to be Ninth Graders, in identical club jackets with WHEELS lettered on the back. They were strolling casually with their arms locked, holding up the crowd behind them. It made for a gigantic traffic jam. But nobody dared to push through, or even tried to get around them. The three WHEELS were laughing and horsing around and having a great time. Then they spotted somebody coming from the other direction.

He was a tall kid, but skinny and frail looking, with like zero muscle tone. And he was wearing tortoise rim glasses that made him look a bit doofie. You know the type that goes through life with a "Kick Me Hard" sign taped on his back and the word "Victim" written all over his face.

The WHEELS changed direction, attaching themselves to him, and they headed back down the hall in my direction.

"Well, well, well, if it isn't Jakove the Jack-Off!" one of them said loud enough for everybody to hear.

"Oh, Harrison," another one mocked with a falsetto voice, "How are things in Fairyland, Jack-Off?"

They circled him like sharks, but he didn't answer. He tried to ignore them, but I could see it in his eyes, a mixture of fear, contempt and resignation.

"Don't you like us, gayboy? You never have anything to say to us."

Harrison Jakove held his books tighter in his hands and against his body, bracing for what he knew was about to come. "I would stop and engage you in conversation guys, but I'll be late for my next class. And besides, I'd have to explain the meaning of too many words to you."

His remark made me laugh, as the four of them stopped right in front of me.

"You know," the biggest WHEEL said, "I get the feeling that the our pal Jack-Off doesn't like all the attention we show him."

He laid his fat and sweaty hand on Jakove's shoulder and spun him around. Jakove tried to break away, but it was too late. He was caught and the other WHEELS began turning him around and around in a circle, faster and faster, until he was too dizzy to stand up. There was a crowd around them laughing and cheering. I felt really sorry for the kid.

"Just leave me alone, will you?" he protested as he staggered around. But that wasn't to be. Somebody put out a foot and somebody else slapped at his books, and Jakove was down on the floor in one direction, and his notebooks, loose-leaf and biology book in the other. I was standing right there practically pinned to the lockers.

"Break it up!" Mr. Gentile yelled from across the hall. He was trying to push his way into the middle of things. "Are you all right, Harrison?" He helped him to his feet.

"I think so, Mr. Gentile." His glasses were crooked on his face. "But my books? My homework?" They were scattered all over the hall.

Mr. Gentile glared at the WHEELS. "Galante," he said to the biggest one. He was trying hard to control his voice, but the veins in his forehead were sticking out.

"What are you looking at me for? I didn't do it. Ask anybody." He turned to the kids around him. They were all shaking their heads.

"Pick up those books, Galante. You and your friends pick up every one of those papers."

"What for? We didn't do it. This kid is a spaz. He can't even walk straight." Everybody laughed.

"I said pick them up!"

Then the second bell rang.

"That's the warning bell, Mr. Gentile. We wouldn't want to be late for class. Will you write us all late passes?" Galante asked with unmistakable sarcasm.

"Just get out of here, Galante. Everybody, go to class!" Mr. Gentile was practically yelling and the crowd broke up. He picked up some of the papers and handed them to Harrison Jakove.

When everything got back to normal, Mr. Gentile showed me to the rest of my classes.  He apologized for what had happened and he hoped it wouldn't affect my opinion of Vanderville.

"Vanderville is really a good school," he said when we ended up back in his office, " with a very few exceptions."

I started school the next day.

# Chapter Two
# "The Library"

It took me a little time to fit into the routine at Vanderville. Since the term had already started, there were a lot of assignments I had to make up, but the teachers were nice, and they all said they'd give me time to catch up. I had a lot of reading to do, but that wasn't really a big problem. I had covered most of the work in the other schools I went to, and many of the books that were required at Vanderville I had already read on my own. Like I said, I'm a pretty intense reader. Sometimes I read three books at a time. Well, not all at once. I start one and put it down and then go to the next, and pretty soon I have three of four books going at the same time. I have a pretty good memory, so it isn't too confusing. Daddy always teases me about leaving a trail of books wherever I've been.

He had started his new job, and he got home every night about six. That gave me plenty of time for myself. I filled it by reading, straightening up the house and getting things ready for dinner. I'm a pretty fair cook, nothing fancy, but I know how to make a bunch of different things, stuff Daddy likes. Other times I practiced dancing.

Daddy helped with the housework whenever he could. He's very good like that. And he helped me with my homework every night. We had fun fixing up the house together. We had brought some of our own personal things. We didn't have much, and we put up the family pictures so it would seem like home. The house was already furnished, so we didn't need any furniture. It's funny and a little sad, but just about all of my life I've lived in furnished apartments with other people's things. That makes it easier for us to pick up and move on, but it's kind of creepy always sleeping on somebody else's mattress all the time. And the scratches and the dents on the furniture belong to somebody else. It's like there isn't any record of my own personal history. I think that's why when I grow up I'm going to live in one house, in one place, and fill it up with my own things, and never move away.

At school I kept to myself, for the most part. There were a couple of girls who sat with me to eat lunch on the first day, but I guess just sitting at the table wasn't their idea of having a good time, so after a while they moved on. Harrison Jakove was in my English class. It didn't take me long to discover that he was the smartest kid in the class, maybe even in the whole school. Mrs. Turnbull, the teacher, knew it too. I could tell that she really liked Harrison. And she was strict, so she didn't allow any fooling around in class, and she didn't let anybody pick on Harrison while he was there.

The first time I spoke to him was in the school library. I was trying to catch up on some algebra during study hall. If there's one thing I hate, it's math. I really stink at word problems, so I was struggling through a whole page of them. He kind of sneaked up on me, but he wasn't really sneaking. He was wearing shoes with rubber soles, so he didn't make much noise, just a little squeaky sound now and then, whenever he turned on the tile floor.

I was totally engrossed in a distance problem. My face was close to the paper, when I heard these faint chirps, like a family of little birds, and then the chair on the other side of the table pulled out with a loud scrape. I didn't look up. I just raised my eyes a little.

He took a long time getting settled in his seat. First he unfastened the rubber strap that held his books together, and then he spread them out on the table in front of him. He shuffled some pages and clicked his ballpoint pen a couple of times and then there was silence.

I was having a hard time understanding the concept of the problem I was working on, and suddenly I was aware that my tongue was sticking out of my mouth. It's something I do unconsciously when I'm thinking. It's dumb, I know, but I can't help it sometimes.

He looked over at the problem I was struggling with and cleared his throat. "Forty-seven miles," he whispered.

I lifted my head from the paper and pulled my tongue back into my mouth. "Excuse me?"

"The answer to that problem you're working on is forty-seven miles. That's when the car with the police S.W.A.T. team catches up with the truck full of terrorists." He pushed his glasses up from the end of his nose where they had slid, and rolled his head around on his neck until I heard it crack.

Close up like we were, I was able to study his face. His hair was curly and thick, and kind of piled up on the top of his head. His ears stuck out a little and his glasses slid to the tip of his nose again. He had a big nose. Not gigantic, I mean, but rather large for the size of his face. And he wore black-rimmed glasses that kept slipping down and he kept pushing up. I tried not to stare at him. His neck and face were covered with blotches, and some milky stuff that looked like medicine. He was well into what adults call the "awkward stage" of adolescence. Now that might sound like an insult, but I don't mean it to be. He was just into the process of becoming whatever it was he was going to be. Me too, for that matter. But besides all that, he was kind of cute, and he had terrific hazel eyes, honest and clear, and flecked with yellow edges.

"Oh," I said, and went back to my figuring, counting on my fingers until I got the answer myself. "You're right, forty-seven miles. Thanks."

"We're in the same English class." He unhooked his loose-leaf binder and took out some pages.

"I know. Mrs. Turnbull."

More red blotches started on his face and down his neck, disappearing under the collar of his shirt. He was aware of them, because he started to scratch. He lifted his paper and covered his face with it so just his eyes were visible behind the reflection of the overhead lights in his glasses.

"My name is Harrison Jakove," he said.

"I know. You're in my English class. Remember?"

"What's the matter with your foot? You have an accident?"

His question was very direct, but I could tell he wasn't trying to make me feel bad. He was just curious. It's funny, but lots of people are curious about those kinds of things. They want to know how somebody got blind or lost an arm or a leg or something. But most people wouldn't dream of asking. Instead they stare when you're not watching, and then they look away when they see you catch them staring. Other times people just try to ignore those things completely, like they don't exist. I guess that's why lots of people ignore me, like I'm invisible, like I don't exist. But I do. Hello. I'm here. And I'm alive.

I don't blame them, really. I guess it makes some people feel uncomfortable being around damaged people. So I didn't mind it when Harrison asked.

"It's not my foot, it's my hip. I was born this way."

"Oh," he said. "Does it hurt much?"

"No, not really. What's the matter with your face?" I asked.

"Oh, you noticed." He slid down a little further in his seat. "Hives. I wasn't born with them, but I blossom whenever I eat certain stuff, or if I get nervous. I have a lot of food allergies. Hives are kind of yukky, but they're only temporary. Gone by tomorrow, I hope, if I put medicine on them. And they're not catchy, so you don't have to worry. When these hives are gone all I'll have to worry about is my normal terminal acne." He smiled a kind of silly smile that made me laugh loud enough for the librarian to put down her copy of The New York Times and frown at us.

"I have work to do," I said. "Why don't we talk later?"

When the period was almost over we were walking together in the hall. "I guess I'll see you in Turnbull's class tomorrow," he said. Then he squeaked off in the opposite direction I was going.

I was half way down the hall when I heard them.

"Hey, hey, hey, it's our lucky day. Jakove the Jack-Off, what do you say?"

I turned around and saw the three WHEELS picking up speed toward Harrison. He stopped short and his shoes made a piercing screech. He was trying to run away, but it was too late. They had him surrounded.

"What's new, omelet face?"

Harrison's books were dumped and kicked out of the rubber strap and along the hall. Harrison tried to defend himself. He stood face to face with the other kid, the WHEEL who had knocked his books out of his hands. Harrison was actually taller than the kid, but he was way out-weighed.

"Why don't you just–"

"Just what, faggot?" He pushed Harrison and his glasses flew off and hit the floor. Then, in another second, Harrison was on the floor.

I hurried down the hall, running as fast as I could, and I was yelling. I could hear myself screaming. "Leave him alone, you stupid morons!" It was my voice, but it sounded like it was coming from somebody else. I was so mad I was crying.

"Hey, get a load of the cripple," one of them said. "Jack-Off and a crip. What a great pair."

And they all laughed.

"Oh, Harrison, you sly devil you. We thought you liked boys."

They punched him in the arm and gave him noogies on the top of his head. One WHEEL smushed his face. That was when the bell rang and everybody came running out into the hall.

Harrison was still on the floor when I reached him. His books and his papers were everywhere. The kids were stepping on them and kicking them. They were stepping on him, like he wasn't even there. I tried to help him up, but nobody else even stopped. Then somebody stomped on his glasses and smashed them. It was awful. I felt so sorry for Harrison. I was really crying. There were hot tears running down my face.

All of a sudden Harrison was wiping my tears with his handkerchief. In spite of everything that had happened to him, he was comforting me.

"Don't cry. You'll be all right."

But I couldn't stop crying. "Your glasses. They broke your glasses."

"Aw, it's all right." He was patting me on the shoulder. "I have another pair. In fact, I have two other pairs. This kind of stuff happens to me all the time. My mother has stock in the eye glass company practically."

I couldn't help it. The way he said it was so funny that I started to laugh. Then Harrison started to laugh. And all the kids in the hall looked at us like we were weird, sitting there on the floor with all those papers around us, laughing hysterically.

That was the day I knew I hated the WHEELS.

# Chapter Three
## "Scotty Dwyer"

In every school I've been to I've noticed that the kids bunch up in groups. The same kinds of kids have a way of finding each other, and they hang out together. Like the saying goes, "Birds of a feather." The names of the groups may be different from school to school, but the kids are pretty much the same, jocks, preppies, greasers and freaks. The jocks are on all the teams. The preppies join the clubs and go out for student council. The greasers, burnouts they were called in California, are the throwbacks who smoke in the bathrooms, write on the walls and drag their knuckles on the ground when they walk through the halls. In Vanderville that was the WHEELS! The freaks were people like Harrison Jakove, and me. Dexters, spazes, wimps, fags, nerds, geeks, dorks. They had lots of names for kids like us.

There were only three WHEELS. Choo-Choo Cooper, whose real name was Lester, Frank LeBeau, who was called "Masher," because that's what he did to kids in the halls, and Carmine Galante. He was the founder and the leader of the WHEELS. He had moved out to Vanderville from New York City. He was older than the other kids in school, sixteen, and he was bigger than most. He had hair on his chest that he liked to show off, and there was some growing on his knuckles too. He had a self-inflicted tattoo, a blue cross, on his right hand. He was dirty and grubby, a real charmer, who had been left back, at least once.

Carmine Galante ruled the WHEELS, and the WHEELS seemed to rule Vanderville. They rolled through the halls without having to answer to anyone. They cut classes, extorted money from kids in the lunchroom, scribbled graffiti on the walls, smoked outside between classes, and they could be found at the center of trouble wherever it was. Nobody did anything to stop them. Most of the teachers had a way of not seeing them. Even Mr. Fagan, the nervous principal, avoided dealing with them.

The WHEELS had a band of admirers, kids who wanted to be WHEELS, or kids who didn't want to be victims of the WHEELS.  So, wherever the WHEELS went, crowds seemed to follow.

They were on the other side of the cafeteria, in a tight circle, with a bunch of the other kids.  They were very visible in their satin club jackets, hatching some kind of scheme.  I could tell.  But if I had noticed them, they were also very aware of me.  I guess calling them "stupid morons" had made me a target for some of their pranks, because from time to time bits of food and stuff came sailing across the cafeteria and landed on my table.  Mr. Eberly, the lunch duty teacher, didn't see them throwing things because he was too busy trying to mooch a free ice cream from the lunch lady behind the counter.

When a gooey bit of mashed potatoes and peas landed in a pile in front of me, I considered dumping the rest of my lunch in the garbage pail and going up to the library. But I didn't want the WHEELS to have the satisfaction of chasing me out.  It was a matter of pride.  I'm not the bravest person in the world.  I cry when I get hurt, and sometimes just when I get mad.  I only wanted to get on with my life at Vanderville.  I wanted to ignore the WHEELS, and I wanted them to ignore me in return.  Then, when a grape squished off the top of my head, I seriously began considering how I might be able to hurt them a little.  I knew it wouldn't solve anything, and it would probably make matters worse for me, but it sure would have made me feel better to get even.

I tried to pretend they didn't exist as best as I could.  I opened the book I was reading, William Golding's The Lord of the Flies. It's this really terrific story about a bunch of boys who are marooned on this island and how savage they become when there aren't any adults around to tell them what to do.  The adults are all off somewhere killing each other in a war.  The story was also made into a movie, twice, but the book is so much better.

The hysteria on the other side of the cafeteria grew, and a wild cheer went up.  I couldn't help looking over.  At first I didn't know what everybody was carrying on about. I half expected something else, like a chair, to come flying across the room.  Then I realized what was happening.  A little person, a dwarf, had been pushed out of the center of the circle with a long rope tied around his neck.  He was wearing a pointed hat made out of newspaper and he looked like a court jester.

The other kids, encouraged by the WHEELS, were laughing at him, telling him to jump around on the tables, throwing things at him. The dwarf turned a cartwheel and lost his hat, but somebody pressed it back on to his head, and Carmine Galante tugged real hard on the rope. That made the kid jump, just like a monkey on a string.

The other kids clumped around Carmine Galante and the dwarf, and then they opened up a pathway, as everyone headed in my direction. Mr. Eberly had stepped outside the cafeteria, so pretty soon kids were standing on the tables and the seats to get a better view of what was going to happen. Even the women who were serving food stopped what they were doing to watch. There was a lot of hooting and yelling.

The dwarf ran out to the end of his rope, charging the kids that were closest to him. He showed his teeth and growled like a captured animal, swinging his arms wildly. Some of the kids ran away, but others caught him and flung him back into the circle. Carmine Galante was pulling him and practically dragging him by the rope. And the whole time everybody but the dwarf was having a great time.

It all reminded me of a scene I once saw in an old movie called The Hunchback of Notre Dame. A really famous old-time actor named Charles Laughton played the part of Quasimodo, the hunchback. He lived in this church, Notre Dame, in Paris. He was so ugly that all the people were afraid of him, so they teased him and laughed at him and did mean things to hurt him. The priest kept Quasimodo in the church and cared for him and fed him, and in return, the hunchback worked for the priest as the bell ringer in the church tower. Once the people caught Quasimodo and dressed him up and humiliated him. It was a sad story. In the end the hunchback died for the love of this beautiful girl. I cried when I saw it.

Well, when I saw what they were doing to that dwarf, it reminded me of the movie. He was fighting the crowd the whole time, flailing around, still wearing that silly paper hat. And the dwarf was smiling, but it wasn't a real smile. It was more of a grimace, like there was a lot of pain under it all.

Carmine Galante led him right up to my table. "Sic her!" he ordered and the dwarf jumped up on the table in front of me.

He snarled and hopped around and bared his teeth and growled. I was so scared, but I didn't move. I couldn't. And I couldn't help staring at him and thinking about poor

Charles Laughton. He stopped jumping long enough to put his face so close to mine, I could smell chocolate on his breath.

"What's the matter, sugar?" he hissed at me through his teeth. The sound of his voice, the look in his eyes, made my hair stand up. "Didn't you ever see a freak before?"

Everybody laughed. I lowered my eyes. They were filling up. I could feel it. I collected my things and started through the door. Mr. Eberly was coming in as I was going out. He said something about a pass. I couldn't understand him. I was too upset. I just turned and saw the dwarf still standing there wearing his silly hat and the rope, watching me walk out. He had such a strange look on his face. Then he pulled the hat from his head, and I left.

Once I was in the hall I didn't know where to go. When a hall duty teacher saw me standing there crying, she brought me to the nurse's office.

"It's all right," I tried to tell the nurse, Mrs. Lefkowitz. "I'm not sick. I'm just a little upset." But she stuck a thermometer into my mouth anyway. School nurses are always doing that. Then she asked me my name and looked up my records on a sheet that said "Confidential" on the top. It was a list of students with special medical problems.

"Are you hurt?" she asked with a more sympathetic tone. "Does your hip bother you?"

"I'm fine," I said. "Really, I am."

But she didn't want to take any chances because she told me to lie down on a cot in this little cubicle. There was a whole bunch of cots in little cubicles, some empty and some with kids lying on them. I really didn't want to, but Mrs. Lefkowitz insisted. I guess she was afraid of getting sued if she did the wrong thing.

I was sitting up on the cot waiting for the bell to ring when Harrison came into the nurse's office. When he saw me he stuck his head through the open curtain.

"Hi," he said. He pushed his glasses up from the tip of his nose. They were held together in the middle with a band-aid. "What are you in here for?" He came over and leaned on the cot.

"Nothing. What about you?"

"Nothing too. I work here. I mean, I'm in here so much, Mrs. Lefkowitz figured I might as well work here. I have an excuse from gym because I had Rheumatic Fever when I was a kid. So instead of sitting around in a smelly gym and aggravating my allergies, I come here and help out. Sometimes I even eat my lunch here, that way I don't have to go to the cafeteria either."

"That's where I just came from." I told Harrison about what had happened at lunch.

"The dwarf is Scotty Dwyer. He lives around the corner from me. We used to be best friends when we were both little. But he really changed in sixth grade. And he got mean here at the junior high. Now I just try to stay away from him."

"Is he a WHEEL?" I asked.

"Nah. They just play around with him like a toy, and get him to do dumb things. They keep promising him if he passes their initiation he can be in the club. But I wouldn't bet on that ever happening. So, I guess you could call him a training WHEEL. It's too bad though that he hangs around with those guys. I'm kind of surprised that he lets them do the things they do. He used to be smart, and write poems and stuff. He even won a prize once when we were in grammar school."

When the bell rang, Mrs. Lefkowitz came in and asked me if I felt well enough to go to class. It was eighth period, the last one, and I had Ninth Grade Chorus with Mr. Borst. Harrison picked up my books and walked me to the Chorus Room. I really liked Harrison.

Later, at the dismissal bell, the halls were full of kids fighting to get their coats out of their lockers and catch the buses before they left. Some kids watched as I came up the hall and they laughed. I figured I was their entertainment for the day. But when I got to my locker there was a different lock on it, and I couldn't get it open. Then they really started laughing.

I knew it had to be the WHEELS. Changing the lock was such a rotten thing to do. My coat and things were in the locker, and by the time I got a custodian to open it, the bus would be gone for sure and I'd have to walk home in the sleet and rain. I gave my locker a good kick, but that wasn't what I wanted to kick.

The custodian's office was at the farthest end of the school, in an annex. I was never there before. It took me a long time to get there because I kept getting lost trying to find the place.

The halls were empty and it was dark and kind of spooky when I finally turned down the right corridor. I could hear the squeak of sneakers from the track team running practice laps through the halls, up and down the stairs. They did that whenever the weather outside was bad. And somebody was using the weight room. I heard the clank of the equipment off in the distance. But the rest of the building was quiet.

"Psssst!" I heard from behind me, but I didn't turn around. "Psssst! Hey, Sugar!" It was Scotty Dwyer. He was standing partially behind one of the crates that was in the hall. He was up high over my head, like he was just casually waiting for me to come by.

"You frightened me," I said. I thought the WHEELS were with him, but he was alone. "And my name isn't 'Sugar,' so don't call me that. In fact, don't talk to me at all."

He jumped down next to me. He was very agile and light on his feet. "I'm sorry," he said. "I didn't mean to scare you. I just wanted to say I'm sorry for what happened today in the cafeteria. I didn't know you were a cripple until I saw you walk out. I didn't realize you are a freak too."

"I'm not a *cripple*," I said. "And I certainly don't consider myself a *freak*!" I started to walk around him. "Now if you'll kindly excuse me, I have to get a custodian to take off the lock you and your friends put on my locker."

He held the open lock in his hand. "I already took it off. It's a little too late, I know. I'm sorry you missed your bus." He looked very apologetic. "You won't have to worry, I won't bother you anymore. I promise."

I turned around and faced him. I just had to say something to him. "How could you let them do that to you? The way they dragged you around. I've seen people treat animals better. You mustn't like yourself very much to let the WHEELS-"

"What do you know?" he said. He was angry. He balled up his fists. "What the hell do you, or anybody, know about me and how I feel?"

"I just know that I think too much of myself to let anybody make a puppet on a string out of me."

"Yeah, well–" He started to say something else, but he never finished. His face got real red. Then he just stepped behind the crate and disappeared. I went to see where he was hiding, but he was gone, like he had vanished into thin air.

I had to walk home two miles in the cold rain. I was soaking wet when I got in the door, and it was pretty late. I started dinner, but I wasn't very hungry. When my father got home I told him I wasn't feeling well and I went to bed. Maybe I did have a fever, because I tossed and turned and I didn't sleep much that night. I kept seeing Scotty Dwyer, and the way he looked in the cafeteria with that hat and rope. And I couldn't help thinking about the hunchback of Notre Dame. In my nightmares the two of them were the same.

# Chapter Four
## "The Visit"

I was sick for a couple of days. I got a bad case of tonsillitis from walking home in the rain and the cold. It was almost two miles from school to the house and walking took me a long time. While I was home alone from school, I cleaned the house, read, practiced my dance exercises, and watched daytime TV. I was watching a rerun of *Gilligan's Island*. It was the one where the Professor mixed a potion that Gilligan accidentally drank and became invisible. When he disappeared, Skipper and everybody thought something terrible had happened to him. They were all sorry they were so mean to Gilligan when he was alive. They were all crying and carrying on, even Mr. Howell and Lovie his wife, when the telephone rang.

"Hello?" I said.

"Hello, um, Hildy? This is Harrison Jakove."

"Hi, Harrison." I was really happy and surprised to hear his voice. Usually the only phone calls I got were wrong numbers, or people trying to sell aluminum siding or something.

"When you weren't in Turnbull's class I asked the nurse. She said you were sick. I hope it isn't anything serious."

"No, just my tonsils. I get it all the time. But my father said I should stay home until Monday and rest."

"That's terrific. I mean, not that you're sick, but that it's not serious." There was a pause when neither of us knew what to say. I guess Harrison wasn't used to talking to people on the phone either. "Well, um, I hate to be the messenger with bad news, but I have homework for you."

"Great. I called this morning and asked Mr. Gentile to send it."

"You really must be sick to call up and ask for homework. Even I don't do that!"

"I'm just caught up and I don't want to fall behind again."

There was another pause. "I could bring it over?" It sounded like a question. "If that's all right with you."

"Sure," I said. "I'd be happy for the company."

"Great. I'll be over as soon as school's out."

I gave him directions and when he hung up I rushed around and straightened things up again. Harrison was the first boy to visit me. In fact, Harrison was the first person to visit. And even though I didn't think of him like a boyfriend or anything, it was kind of exciting, and I wanted to make a good impression.

At ten after three the doorbell rang. When I opened the door Harrison was standing there with some schoolbooks under his arm. He was wearing a brown leather hat with fur earflaps, the kind old-time aviators used to wear. One of the earflap straps was flipped up over the top of his head. I couldn't help laughing when I saw him. He looked so wrinkled, not just his clothes, but Harrison himself. Even his glasses were crooked.

"Hi," he said and smiled back. "Sorry I'm late, but I was delayed a little." The only thing that wasn't funny about Harrison was the bruise under his left eye.

"What happened to you? Your eye?"

His hand went up to feel the spot that was puffed. "Well," he said, "I kind of ran into my locker. It's nothing really."

"It wouldn't have anything to do with the WHEELS by any chance, would it?"

"Well, now that you mention it, the WHEELS were kind of standing near my locker when I kind of ran into it."

"Come on in and put some ice on it." I led him into the living room and went into the kitchen for an ice cube.

He looked all around the place. "Nice house. Plenty of room. Not a lot of furniture. I like that. My house is crammed full of furniture. There isn't even room to walk."

I handed him the ice in a plastic bag. He took it and put it on his eye and sat on the couch. He laid the books on the coffee table.

"Well," I said after a while, "what are you going to do about that?"

"Nothing. It'll go away." He balanced the ice on his eye and picked up the brass ballerina sculpture from the table and studied it. "It looks worse than it is. It doesn't hurt really. Not a lot anyway. I've had worse, believe me. My mother gets a discount from the doctor."

I guess it showed on my face, how I was feeling.

"Don't worry about it."

"I mean the WHEELS. Harrison, you just have to do something about them. You can't keep letting them beat you up. You don't own enough pairs of glasses. And the next things they'll start breaking are your bones. It makes me so mad the way the WHEELS keep right on rolling along, and you have to sit there balancing a bag of ice on your black eye. What are you going to do?"

"You mean what are we going to do? You've become a target too. I heard about what they did to your locker. The WHEELS are full of fun stuff like that. And always when it's raining out, or snowing. And that's just the beginning. Wait until they fill your locker up with Jello!" He straightened his head and caught the ice when it fell. "Or dog poop!" His eye was really getting black and blue, like in the movies. The earflap on his hat came down. "It took me a week to clean it out when they did it to me. And on damp days you can still smell it."

"How did you know about my locker? Who told you?"

"Scotty. He came over to my house the other day, just like that, to hang around the way he used to. He also filled me in on his version of what happened in the cafeteria. Carmine Galante put the word out for everybody to make your life as miserable as mine. Scotty also said he was sorry for what he did. And that he told the WHEELS that he didn't want anything to do with it." He stood up. "Boy, things sure were a lot simpler when I was young, and before Carmine Galante moved into my life."

"But can't you tell somebody? Your parents? Mr. Gentile or the principal?"

"My parents have their own problems. I think they're getting ready for a divorce. And there isn't much anybody can do at school. Everybody is afraid of the WHEELS. So I guess I'll just have to tough it out." He pointed to the picture on the wall. "Who's that? Your sister? She's pretty."

"That's my mother."

"What's she all dressed up for?"

"Swan Lake. That's a ballet costume. She was a dancer."

"She sure is great looking. When does she come home from work?" He looked out the window.

"She doesn't. She's dead."

"Oh," he said, and turned around to me. "She looks too young to be dead. What did she die from?"

"An accident," I said. I really didn't want to go into all the details. "In her car. It happened when I was just a kid." I picked up one of my books from the coffee table and opened it to the page that was marked.

"I'm sorry," he said. "My mother is still alive. She works at J C Penny." I knew he meant it to make me feel better. The way he said it made me laugh, and Harrison smiled. "Well, I have to go, Hildy. I'm sure glad you're feeling better. Thank you for the ice." He snapped the straps of his earflaps under his chin. "I guess I'll see you in school Monday."

"Thanks, Harrison." I walked him to the door and watched as he peddled down the street on his bike. It was a contraption he had put together from odds and ends, the perfect bike for him. "Take care of yourself, and be careful," I called after him.

All weekend I tried to think of a solution for Harrison's problems. And I thought about me becoming a new target for the WHEELS. There had to be some way to defend ourselves.

# Chapter Five
# "Pep Day"

The day I went back to school was Pep Day.

Everybody in school was excited because all of the class periods were shortened for a special sports assembly program at the end of the day. Besides missing some class time, Pep Day was a great excuse for everyone acting a little crazier than usual all day long.

Vanderville is a *real* sports school, probably more than any other school I've been to. There are a bunch of trophies in the showcase outside the Main Office, for football, soccer, track, cheer leading and everything. Even the Home Economics Department had a trophy on display for a quilting bee that they won. And on Pep Day all the jocks are allowed to wear their team jerseys around the school.

At the end of eighth period Mr. Borst brought the chorus to the gym. It was a madhouse, with the teachers running around trying to settle things down, and paper airplanes flying all over the place. I saw Harrison sitting with his class across the gym floor. He was looking for me too, and he waved when he saw me.

Mr. Fagan was standing by the microphone waiting for things to get quiet enough for him to talk. It was kind of pathetic, you know, because the assembly got quiet until Mr. Fagan opened his mouth. Then everybody started up again, hooting and hollering, clapping their hands, cheering and stomping their feet.

There was a big commotion from somewhere behind me, way up on the bleachers. Carmine Galante and the other two WHEELS were at the center of it, of course. They were leading the other kids, getting them going, settling everybody down, and then starting it all over again, laughing and having a great time.

That went on for about five minutes, and no one could stop it. Finally Mr. Goldstein, the athletic director, pulled the microphone right out of Mr. Fagan's hands and blew his whistle directly into it. Everybody grabbed their ears, even Mr. Fagan.

Mr. Goldstein was mad. He yelled into the microphone, "You people better settle down! You kids up there," he pointed toward the WHEELS, "sit down and shut up! Everybody quiet down, and that's a direct order!" He sounded like a Marine drill instructor.

The crowd got quiet right away, and Mr. Goldstein handed the microphone back to Mr. Fagan. The principal smiled and cleared his throat. Then he went on and on about Vanderville Junior High School. He said it was a proud school, proud of its athletes, and proud of its record of achievement on the "athletic field of honor." That's what he called it. "The athletic field of honor," he said, "where young Americans test their mettle every day, and build character, and gird their loins to meet the challenge of a competitive world." He sure took the long way to get where he was going.

During the time that I was at Vanderville Mr. Fagan never seemed to say anything simply. And he had a monotone voice, and a little lisp that made him spray all of his S's into the microphone. Hardly anybody listened to him for more than a minute, and those that did usually made fun of him. I felt sorry for Mr. Fagan in a way.

Well, pretty soon most of the kids turned him off and started talking again. A low murmur, like the sound inside a seashell, started building up and up, until it got impossible to hear what he was saying.

Another blast from Mr. Goldstein's whistle made us all jump again. It produced another deathly silence, and poor Mr. Fagan lisped on.

"And certainly, without any further ado, it behooves me to introduce at this time, the highly successful coaches, who are most certainly eager to introduce their teams–"

A paper clip came winging from the bleachers from behind me, and it bounced at Mr. Fagan's feet. It produced a wave of laughter, followed by three more paper clips in rapid succession. Mr. Fagan was under fire and the paper clips came in like a barrage of artillery shells! Poor Mr. Fagan flinched every time one landed, but he kept on talking. The teachers scanned the kids looking for the culprits, trying to restore order. From the path that the paper clips took, I knew exactly where they were coming from.

Then somebody's athletic supporter snapped out of the audience and landed right on the microphone, and even Mr. Goldstein's whistle couldn't restore order.  It was chaos.

When the dismissal bell finally rang at the end of the assembly, the kids filed out of the gym, except for the WHEELS.  Mr. Goldstein had headed them off before they could escape.  He had the three of them in the back corner of the gym, outside his office.  He was steaming mad.  His face was all red and his hands were two fists.  It looked like he was having a hard time controlling himself.  I was waiting for the crowd by the exits to thin out a little before I left, so I saw it all and I heard what he was saying.

"I know it was you bums!" he shouted.  "If I was the principal of this school, you three would be out on your tails, locked up!  You're garbage!  Cancer!"  His voice was so loud it filled the whole gym.

The WHEELS weren't saying anything, just looking at one another or at the floor.  Carmine Galante had a smirk on his face, and that really made Mr. Goldstein boil.

"Galante, you don't belong with normal kids.  You're dirt!  This school was a decent enough place until you got here."

The smirk on his face changed and he got all red.  "You got no right to talk to me like that, Mr. Goldstein-"

"Right?"  Mr. Goldstein reached out and grabbed him by the front of his WHEELS jacket.  "What do you know about right, Galante?  You're a criminal.  A felon.  You don't belong in school.  You ought to be off somewhere breaking rocks, doing hard time!"

Carmine Galante's face got real white as Mr. Goldstein pulled him up off the floor so that only his toes were touching.  For a second he thought Mr. Goldstein was going to hit him, and so did I.  But Mr. Goldstein just shook him a little until a button popped off his shirt.  Then he let him go.

"You can't do that to me.  I didn't do nothing to you, and you got no right to put your hands on me-"

"'Can't,' Galante?  I just did.  And what are you going to do about it, chickenshit?  I'm not one of the little kids you and your bum friends push around.  You're out of your league now.  But any time you think you're man enough and you want to give it a try, the three of you, you know where to find me."

"I could get you in big trouble. I could sue you. If I tell my father-"

"Tell your father, Galante," Mr. Goldstein said in a low voice that was even scarier than when he yelled. "Because I'd like to meet him. I'd like to see the guy who produced a scum bucket like you. Now get your hoodlum asses out of my gym." He smiled and turned his back on the three of them. He kicked the loose button across the gym floor and walked into his office.

Carmine Galante's eyes were narrow slits as he watched Mr. Goldstein go. The other two looked kind of embarrassed for him.

"He can't get away with that!"

"No, he can't."

"I'll show him."

"Yeah."

They went out mumbling. I was real glad they didn't know I was there. And I was even more glad for what Mr. Goldstein did. It was nice to know that somebody at Vanderville wasn't afraid of the WHEELS.

# Chapter Six
## "The Special Bus"

"Hey," I heard from behind me as I was walking through the South Corridor to my school bus. It was Scotty Dwyer. "Wait up." He came running up to me. "Where have you been? I haven't seen you at lunch all week."

"Sick," I said coolly, "from walking home in the rain. And if it's any of your business, I don't eat my lunch in the cafeteria any more. Now, if you'll excuse me, I have a bus to catch."

He handed me a miniature Mars Bar. I just looked at it. I wasn't sure of his motives.

"It's okay. Take it. It's left over from Trick or Treat. Take it. I got more." He followed me outside to the bus.

I didn't ride the regular school bus every day. Because it took me a long time to get out of the building, a lot of times the regular buses were already gone. So sometimes I rode the special bus. Mr. Gentile made arrangements for me and got me a pass for the whole year. He said because of my hip problem I was automatically entitled to ride on it anytime. It would even pick me up in the morning if I wanted.

The kids at Vanderville called the special bus the "Weird Wagon" or the "Tard Cart" because it was usually full of kids from Special Ed, as well as the kids that had broken arms and legs and stuff. At Vanderville there was always a bunch of kids on crutches or with parts of their bodies in casts. When I got outside there was a lineup of them waiting to get on the bus. The kids with casts weren't the regulars. They only rode the bus while their body parts were recovering.

The Special Ed kids rode the bus *every* day. I got to know most of the kids. One girl, Victoria, had Down's Syndrome. And another girl, Jennifer, was brain damaged at birth. They were really sweet. The two of them always sat together in the back of the bus holding hands, because they were afraid of the other kids who teased them and called them "tards" and stuff. It made me mad the way the so-called normal kids acted toward them. And it made me sad to see how insensitive people can be. I found riding on the special bus kind of depressing, so on nice days I chose to walk the two miles. But on this particular afternoon it was cold and I didn't really want to aggravate my tonsils again.

"Hey, you know," Scotty said, "I'm really, *really* sorry for what happened. And I haven't bothered you again, have I? I'd like to be your friend." He took my books and tried to help me up the steps to the bus. He was being so nice, but I still didn't trust him.

"And where do you think *you're* going, Scott Dwyer?" the bus driver demanded. She put her big arm out to bar him from getting on the bus.

"I still have a pass to ride this bus, Mrs. Vogel." He took out his wallet and showed her the wrinkled and folded piece of paper. The writing was faded and hard to read.

"Pass or no pass, I'm not putting up with any more of your shenanigans on *my* bus. You get off right this minute or I'm going to call for a teacher." She looked out the window for some help.

Scotty's face turned red. "It's all right, Mrs. Vogel. I don't want to cause you any trouble. I just want to ride on the bus. I'll be good. I *promise.*"

She eyed him suspiciously and then she looked at me. Finally she pulled her arm back and let him through. "But just remember, young man, one belch, or any other bodily sound, one foul word, a mumbled vulgarity, just one, and I'll throw you right out into the gutter." Mrs. Vogel was a big woman and I had little doubt that she could do just that.

"I'll be good," he said again.

Mrs. Vogel turned her attention to me and the frown that creased her face disappeared. "I think Scott Dwyer has a girlfriend. But you just watch out for him, honey. He can be *very* fresh, and you seem like a nice girl." She laughed. Scotty's face got redder.

"Sounds like you caused *her* a little trouble too," I said when we were seated.

"A little."  He was uneasy, looking around at the rest of the kids.  "I don't like riding this bus."  He stared at Victoria and Jennifer.  "I don't like being with freaks like them.  They make me nervous."  He made a horrible face and growled at them.

"Stop that!  And why do you call them that?"

"They're retards."  He made another face.

The girls just turned away from him.  Scotty was about to say something else, but he saw Mrs. Vogel watching him in the rearview mirror.  Then he looked out the window and quickly ducked down under his seat.

"What's the matter?"  I asked.

"There's somebody I don't want to see me."

Choo-Choo Cooper was walking toward the bus.  He came right up to the window where we were sitting and banged on it.  Scotty made believe he didn't hear him.

"Hey, Dwyer," he said through the glass.  "You riding the Weird Wagon again? Come on, don't play games.  I know you're in there.  We saw you get on with the crip."

Scotty crawled out from under the seat.  "What do you want?"      "Business. WHEELS business.  Carmine is waiting across the street.  Come on!"

"I can't today.  I," he looked at me, "have something I promised to do for my mother.  Tomorrow.  Tell Carmine tomorrow, maybe-"

"Tomorrow's no good."  He stared at me through the window and grinned.  It made me feel so uncomfortable.  "You do what you have to, shrimp, but it's too bad. Carmine's gonna wonder what's more important, getting into the WHEELS or playing footsies with a cripple!"

That really made me mad, but before I could say anything Scotty was up and out of his seat.

"I have to go," he said.  "Just for a second.  Just to explain.  I'll be right back, I promise."  He gave me another candy bar and climbed out of the bus.      That was when Mrs. Vogel shut the door and started the motor.  Scotty turned around and I could see there was a strange expression on his face.  I guess I had a strange look on my face too.  For a second I thought he was going to come back on the bus, but he didn't.  He just watched me until the bus pulled away from the curb.

It was funny. I really didn't know Scotty Dwyer, and he was nothing to me, but I was still sad and angry that he left. I mean, I felt like I was in a tug of war with the WHEELS, and Scotty was in the middle.

# Chapter Seven
## "Call 9-1-1"

All weekend I wrestled with the problem. What should it matter to me if Scotty Dwyer wanted to be one of the WHEELS? What should I care if they treated him like a fool, and he was foolish enough to go along with them? That was his problem, and I had my own problems to deal with.

On Monday morning there was a big row at Vanderville. We had just started Homeroom when Nassau County police cars screeched into the courtyard with their sirens blasting. All the kids were out of their seats and at the windows. And soon the police were all over the building with their walkie-talkies chirping away. It was really something.

Then Mr. Fagan interrupted class with an important announcement over the P.A. First he told the kids, "Stop all work!" and then he instructed the teachers to make *sure* everybody stopped all work and was listening. Everybody was because we thought he was going to tell us what was going on. Instead, he delivered a nine-minute lecture about "acceptable behavior."

He said that he realized that most of the kids in Vanderville were good "school citizens" who obeyed the rules. But there was a small minority, and Mr. Fagan said he knew pretty much who they were, that didn't care about rules and regulations. It was those few kids that he was talking to. Then he went on about the valuable work that the police department did in the county, and how their time ought to be spent arresting criminals. He hinted that an incident, a "heinous act," he called it, had taken place in school over the weekend. He assured us that they were closing in on the suspects at that very second, and they should give themselves up before it was too late, if they knew what was good for them. Then he appealed to any student who had information about the heinous act to come forward with that information as a good school citizen. He ended his speech by announcing that all after-school student activities *might* be canceled unless the culprits surrendered.

When he was finished I didn't really understand what he had been talking about. And neither did any of the other kids in Homeroom. Everybody buzzed with theories and rumors, but it was later, when I spoke to Harrison, that I found out the whole story.

We were in Biology Lab, standing over some poor dead frog with his insides outside and pinned to a lab tray. Harrison and I were "Lab Buddies." We worked it out with the teacher, Mrs. Marshall, and that was great for me. I hated all that dissecting stuff, but Harrison loved it. So he did all the cutting and identifying and the labeling, and I got to share in his grade. He even managed to eat some of his lunch while he did the experiment. He said it was kind of like killing two birds, or frogs in this case, with one stone. And he could stay in the lab longer and not waste time with unimportant stuff. I thought the whole thing was gross.

"Yeah," he said between bites of his egg salad sandwich. "Somebody broke into the Athletic Office over the weekend. They stole some equipment, trashed Mr. Goldstein's office pretty good, and they painted things on the walls and wrote stuff. There were swastikas and some real foul language. But that's not all!" He leaned over closer to me and whispered, "They left a dump right on Mr. Goldstein's desk! Right on his marking book and papers! I overheard the secretaries talking about it in the office. Boy, was Mr. Goldstein teed off. Number one, for what was written on the walls, and number two, for the number *two* on his desk. One of the science teachers said they should send the specimen to the police lab for testing, and then get a sample from every kid in the building and match up the results!"

"Oh my God!" I was no longer interested in the frog.

"Don't get yourself in an uproar. It was just a joke. And besides, it's against the Bill of Rights or something. And scientifically it wouldn't work unless you took all the samples on the same-"

"Harrison, I think I know who it was." From everything he had said, the pieces were fitting into place.

"Who?" His face was up so close to the frog, he was breathing practically pure formaldehyde.

I looked around to make sure that nobody else was listening. Mrs. Marshall wa across the lab setting up the next experiment. All of the other kids were absorbed in thei frogs.

"The WHEELS," I whispered.

"Oh, they were the first ones Mr. Fagan questioned. The three of them had alibis They said they were having a sleepover party at Carmine Galante's. That's what I hear one of the kids say, but I wouldn't be surprised if it *was* them."

"It had to be. I was in the assembly, Harrison, and I heard them say they wer going to get even with Mr. Goldstein. It can't be a coincidence." Harrison hardly lifte his face. Then I let the other shoe drop. "And I think Scotty Dwyer was in it with them!"

That made him stop. He was holding an electric current to the frog's legs, makin them twitch. "Scotty? Break into the office, and do those other things? I don't believ it!" His voice was getting louder and Mrs. Marshall looked over at us. "That's seriou business, Hildy," he whispered. "Are you sure?"

"Well, I'm not positive." I told him what had happened after the Pep Day rall and on the bus with Choo-Choo Cooper.

"Circumstantial evidence," he said, sending the frog into spasms again, "an pretty flimsy. I *know* the WHEELS are capable of stuff like that, but I think Scotty i smart enough to stay out of that kind of trouble. At least I hope he is. This isn't jus cutting class or being rowdy in the halls. This is legal business, with cops, and handcuffs and jail."

"What do you think I should do?"

"Forget about it. Even if it's true, do you really want to get involved? You coul get hurt. Or worse." He pushed his glasses back on his nose. "But if you are right wow!"

I thought about it all day in school. Harrison had a point. It was only circumstantial evidence. There wasn't any real proof. And maybe my bad feelings fo the WHEELS were getting in the way of logical thinking. It could have been anybody who broke into the school. The newspapers were full of stories about crazy people doing crazy things. Besides, Harrison was right, it wasn't any of my business. I was jus passing through Vanderville. What difference did it make to me about some vandalisn to a place I never even heard of six months ago and probably wouldn't remember six months down the road? Let Mr. Fagan handle it, and the police. That's what they were getting paid for. I just wanted to get on with my own life and my own problems. Still I had a bad feeling. My only regret was for Scotty. If he was involved, it was something way over his head.

I left school a little early that day. I had an appointment with a physical therapist in the Nassau County Medical Building. It was something I had agreed to do once a week for my father. I knew it would make him feel better that I was taking steps to improve my condition, even though both of us knew deep down inside that it wouldn't do much good.

I signed out in the Main Office. The secretary smiled when she saw me walk in and she called me "dear." I showed my early dismissal pass to the hall monitor at the door and cut across the front lawn. The county bus that went past the Medical Building stopped right in front of the school, but I had decided to walk. It would take about half an hour and I figured that the exercise would probably be better physical therapy than anything anybody else could do for me.

The afternoon was cold and crisp, and I watched my breath vaporize in front of me like so much smoke. I was pretty deep in thought as I crossed in front of the war monument near the side of the school, so at first I didn't notice anything strange. Then I saw Scotty's head sticking out of the bushes. He ducked down real fast when he saw me, and then when he recognized me he poked his head out again.

"Hildy," he called.

"What are you doing out here?" I asked. "It's freezing." He wasn't wearing a coat. His face was all red. His cheeks and the tip of his nose looked like cherries. He had his hands crammed into his pants pockets and he was shivering. "You'll be lucky if you don't freeze to death!"

"I don't care." He looked over the bushes at the building. "Are the cops still inside?"

"I think they left hours ago. Why?"

"I'm in trouble, Hildy. Big trouble."

"Then I was right," I said and my voice trailed off. "It was you and the WHEELS who broke into Mr. Goldstein's office."

His face turned stark white. "What do you mean? Who told you that?" He started to cry. It was so sad.

"Nobody told me. I just figured it out. The WHEELS, Mr. Goldstein, you."

"You didn't tell anybody?"

"Of course not. Just Harrison."

"Shoot!" He pulled his fists out of his pockets and he was really crying. I felt so sorry for him. "Shoot! Shoot! Shoot! What am I going to do now? I told them I didn't want to do it. I told them! I'm such a jerk. A real jerk!"

"Listen, Scotty, I'm supposed to go for a doctor's appointment now. Instead, why don't you go back inside? It's safe now. Get Harrison, and both of you come to my house right after school. He knows where I live. Maybe the three of us can figure something out." I handed him a tissue. His nose was running.

He wiped his eyes and blew his nose. "Okay," he said.

I watched him slink across the lawn and into a side door.

*  *  *

"I didn't do it, really," Scotty said. The three of us were sitting in the living room, trying to piece together what had happened, and more important, what we were going to do about it.

"I mean, I did help them get into the school. I don't deny that. I squeezed in through the vent window to the Custodian's Office. And then I opened the door for them. So I'm guilty of that part. But I didn't know what they were going to do. And I didn't do any of the damage. Honest. After I let them in I just stood near the door and waited for a chance to get out of there. I swear I didn't do *any* of it." He was crying again.

Nobody said anything for a while. I looked at Harrison and he shook his head.

"What were you thinking of when you agreed to break in? Did they force you? Did they threaten you?" Harrison was working on an angle. "If they forced you, you could plead self-defense, or is that only when you kill somebody?"

"They didn't force me exactly. They said I owed it to the WHEELS for all the things they did for me. Loyalty. And if I didn't help them, I was chicken, and I'd never become a WHEEL."

"And *that* was so important to you? What they said to you was so important? Or what *they* thought about you? Come on, Scotty, you were never like that when you were little."

"I know it sounds dumb and everything, and I don't expect you to understand, but when they said it, it *was* important to me. In case you haven't noticed it," he said sarcastically, "I'm a dwarf! The only one at Vanderville! I'm a freak, an oddball! I don't fit in with any of the other kids, and I'm tired of it! At least the WHEELS gave me some status, and the other kids looked up to me."

"The other kids made fun of you," I said. "They treated you like an animal. I saw them in the cafeteria. And the WHEELS are just using you. Don't kid yourself."

Scotty took a deep breath. "Listen, when I was young, when I was in elementary school, it was great. Nobody treated me bad. Everybody thought I was cute and they made a big fuss over everything I did. And I thought it was because of me, because I was special and clever and bright. I believed that people actually liked *me*. And then I grew up. I realized that people were gawking at something that belonged in a menagerie. I could see it in their faces. Even my parents. Even now, I see their guilt. I hear their regrets that I'm a freak, even if they don't say it out loud. 'What did we do that was so wrong that God had to punish us like this?' And then it got worse. I started junior high school, and people stopped just looking and started saying things. Calling me stuff. And I had to put up with all the nasty teasing, even from the kids who used to be my friends in grammar school. And the names. 'Shrimp Boy' and 'Sawed-Off' and 'Half-Pint.' 'Hey, are you Grumpy, or are you just Dopey? Where's Snow White?' I wanted to kill them. And I got it from the teachers too. I hear them making cracks behind my back. And now everybody is looking forward to the high school and dances and dating and stuff. And sex. That's all that I think about. Who's going to want anything to do with a dwarf? Maybe another freak in a sideshow. What's my future? The circus. If I'm lucky and I can get a job as a clown and give people the opportunity to really laugh at me." It all came out in a rush of words. He was so angry that the tears were running down his cheeks. "But that's all right. I hate them all! I wish they'd all die! I wish I'd die!"

"I have a rheumatic heart. I can't play sports and I'm Jewish," Harrison said. "That doesn't mean anything to me, but it bothers some people. They call me names too. 'Wimp,' 'Faggot,' 'Jew Boy,' 'Kike,' 'Christ Killer.' I'm only fourteen years old and I never killed anybody in my life. So I know what it's like. Being different is hard, especially in a world that tries to make everybody the same. But that doesn't mean you have to give up, Scotty, and throw in the towel. History was made by people who were different. People who were different changed the world. Napoleon. Alexander the Great. Right here in this room there are three of us. We have more talent and more intelligence than all of those dopes combined. A shrimp, a cripple and a Jew. It sounds like a great name for a law firm to me."

Scotty laughed for the first time. Harrison put his arm around him. "Don't worry about those other guys. We used to be best friends. And now there's Hildy too. We've got each other."

It was nice the way it happened. We were all hugging and stuff.

"Now," Scotty said, "if we could only take care of this school thing."

Harrison unwrapped a hard candy he took from the candy dish and popped it into his mouth. "It looks to me like this is a clear case of 'The Three Monkeys.'"

"What's that?" I asked.

"Hear no evil, see no evil and speak no evil. Keep our ears, eyes and mouths shut and hope for the best. If you tell on the WHEELS they *may* get expelled, but you'll probably get expelled too. And if you tell you can bet that Carmine Galante will be after your head. So sometimes doing nothing is the best course of action."

"But whatever you do," I added, "you have to say good riddance to the WHEELS once and for all."

Scotty put his head down. "You're right. I never really liked them anyway." He sighed and it was like a weight was taken off his shoulders.

My father came in just as the strategy meeting was breaking up. He looked surprised when he saw the boys.

"Dad, this is Harrison and Scotty, my two friends from school. And this is my father."

"Pleased to meet you," he said, and he watched me walk them out the door.

We were finishing the supper dishes, me washing and Daddy drying, when he brought up the subject of Harrison and Scotty. "That's an interesting collection of friends," he managed. "They look like a couple of real characters, especially the midget-"

"Dwarf," I corrected. "Scotty's not a midget, he's a dwarf. There's a difference you know."

"Dwarf," he responded. He dried some more of the silverware and smiled. "I didn't mean to sound like I was criticizing." He put down the dishcloth and gave me a hug. "I'm glad you made friends, Hildy. With all the moving around we do, sometimes I worry about you. I know it's been tough on you going to all those new schools, doing without the things most girls your age need. And I haven't been much help. I just want you to know that I like your friends. And I love you."

"I know you do, Daddy." I kissed him on the cheek. "And you don't have to worry any more. Harrison, Scotty and me are real good friends. Like three peas in a pod."

# Chapter Eight
## "Holiday Time In The City"

From all the things I've said about Vanderville Junior High School so far, you might get the impression that it was a bad school. It really wasn't. The WHEELS were probably the worst thing about the place. It got so that I started to think of them kind of the way I thought about pimples. I knew they were there, but there wasn't much I could do about them, just hope they'd go away eventually and not leave permanent scars.

Everything else at Vanderville was going well. I made up all of the work I had to make up, with the help of Harrison and Scotty. All of my grades on the first report card were over eighty-five. I made second honor roll.

Outside of school things were even better. Scotty made his formal break with the WHEELS. His "Declaration of Independence," he called it. We helped him write a letter to Carmine Galante and the others, telling them to drop dead, and promising that if the WHEELS ever bothered *any* of us, Scotty would go right to Mr. Fagan with information about the break in. Otherwise, the letter said, he'd keep his mouth shut and mark the incident up to experience. I guess we were pretty lucky because right after that the investigation died down on its own and seemed to go away.

We were free to spend a lot of time together. It was the first time in my life that I had friends or any kind of social calendar. The three of us went everywhere together. They showed me the sights on Long Island. They took me out for McDonald's, to the flea markets and shopping malls, and to the movies.

Once we went to a multiplex cinema, a theater with about six different movies playing. Scotty thought that if we each had a change of jackets, and maybe a pair of glasses and a couple of different hats as a disguise, we could sneak in to see two or three shows for the price of one. But it didn't work. The manager recognized us right away and we got thrown out. I guess we were pretty easy to pick out of a crowd. Anyway, it was fun, and exciting trying.

I was having such a great time that the days were really flying right along. Thanksgiving was over already. Daddy and I spent the holiday alone, just the two of us. Grandma Olga and Grandpa Louis had sent me a plane ticket to Florida, and an invitation to spend the long Thanksgiving weekend with them. But I didn't go. Daddy couldn't get the day after Thanksgiving off, and anyway the invitation didn't include him. He said that I should go if I wanted, but I didn't want to leave him. The holidays can be a lonely and depressing time, especially if you don't have anybody you love to spend them with.

So I called up my grandparents and thanked them for the thought. My grandmother told me to keep the ticket and use it whenever I wanted to visit, or cash it in and buy myself some new clothes with the money. She's always doing stuff like that. She's really a wonderful person, once you get to know her, and there isn't anything she wouldn't do for me. But sometimes she comes on pretty strong. "Damn the torpedoes, full speed ahead!"

I don't think she really meant to slight Daddy, or make him feel bad about Thanksgiving, but there are still some things they haven't worked out between them. Things are better now. When my mother died, Grandma Olga didn't even talk to Daddy for a long time. She blamed him because it happened right after my mother and Daddy had a big fight. My mother got pretty depressed soon after I was born. It's something that sometimes happens to women after they have babies. Post-partum depression it's called and it has to do with hormones or something. Grandma Olga and I talked about it once. She said that things changed for my parents right after I was born, and that my mother and Daddy started to fight a lot. My mother ended their last fight by driving her car into a stonewall. She was going fast. There was an investigation and talk about suicide because they found traces of alcohol and medication in her blood.

I guess my mother was going through a pretty rough time when I was born. Like I said, it happens to a lot of women after they have babies. And I guess the problem with my hip didn't help things. But it still makes me wonder. And it makes me mad at my mother to think that because of one stupid night, Grandma Olga, Grandpa Louis, Daddy, me and everybody in the world were deprived of someone so important. That's when I hate her for what she did to us. And then I feel kind of guilty for feeling that way.

When my grandparents got the news they flew in from Connecticut where they lived. My grandfather used to be a police captain there before he retired. Right after they arrived the investigation was closed and the cause of death was officially listed as accidental.

It was a horrible time for everybody. Soon after the funeral Daddy left. And there was all that legal business when Grandma tried to adopt me and get me to live with her permanently. Of course I was just a baby, so I don't know all the facts. Whenever we talked about my mother, my grandmother always insisted it was an accident. I'm sure she couldn't face the possibility that her beautiful and talented daughter could want to commit suicide. But it's something that I wonder about a lot.

Anyway, that was a long time ago, and like I said, things are better now.

So Daddy and I had Thanksgiving dinner out, a seven-course meal at a fancy restaurant. And then we went to a movie. We had fun together.

The weather changed right after Thanksgiving. It got colder. It didn't snow, but everybody was getting ready for snow, and Christmas vacation. Vanderville put on its best Christmas and Chanukah decorations. In fact, all of Long Island was getting into the holiday spirit. Every day more and more houses were lit up for the season.

One Saturday Harrison, Scotty and I decided to take the Long Island Railroad into the city. I wanted so much to see the big Christmas tree at Rockefeller Center. I had seen it on TV, of course, but never in real life.

Manhattan is such a beautiful place, especially around Christmas. All the store windows are decorated in a competition that makes everybody who sees them a winner. And the crowds are so thick that just walking on the sidewalk is an adventure. There are all these wonderful little white lights in the bare trees along Fifth Avenue that make everything look like a fairy tale come true. On every street corner practically, the vendors are selling roasted chestnuts and stuff, and everywhere musicians are giving free concerts. The sights, the sounds the smells, they are wonderful. There's so much to do. There's nothing like it anywhere in the world.

"Come on," I said, moving along with the crowd, "I want to see everything!" Harrison had grabbed on to my arm so we wouldn't lose him. I couldn't believe it was the first time he had been into Manhattan, living so close.

"Hey, wait for me!" Scotty called. He had wormed his way through the crowd to get a closer look at the animated window displays.

On the steps of St. Patrick's Cathedral we asked somebody to take our picture with the camera I had brought. Then we bought a bag of chestnuts and elbowed our way along to Rockefeller Center. It was so beautiful.

"Hey," Scotty said when he looked down at the people gliding around the rink. He had the biggest grin on his face. "Let's go skating. What do you say?"

Harrison looked at the circle of skaters and wiped his runny nose with the back of his mitten. "Ice skating?" The earflaps of his aviator cap were sticking straight out like wings. "But I never ice skated in my life."

"Me either," I said. "But it'll be fun." I grabbed one end of Harrison's scarf.

"I'll show you how. There's really nothing much to it." Scotty grabbed the other end of the scarf and we pulled Harrison between us toward one of the uniformed attendants.

"Excuse me," I said. "We'd like to skate. Where can we rent skates?"

The attendant was a young guy, a college kid, and he was trying to pick up one of the girls from some tour group or something. At first he was annoyed at the interruption and he looked down his nose at the three of us. Then the expression on his face turned to one of amusement and he called another attendant to check us out. I guess we were a pretty strange sight, holding Harrison between us like he was on a leash. Finally he pointed to a big rental sign and went back to the girls.

"Really," Harrison asked, "do we *have* to do this?" He was laced into his skates, struggling to balance on the carpet, trying desperately to keep his ankles from bending in.

For an instant, I have to admit, I had second thoughts about the idea, but then I decided what the heck. "You have to take some chances in life, Harrison, or it isn't worth it. What's the worse thing that can happen?" I asked, but I didn't really want to know.

"It's simple," Scotty said. "Just try and stay on the blades."

"That's like telling a tight rope walker, 'Just keep your feet on the rope'!" Harrison said.

We certainly were a sight, the three of us, when we finally made it onto the rink. Harrison and I hugged the handrail and each other. We were pathetic, but Scotty was terrific. He could do almost anything on skates. He even skated backwards while he helped us around the rink a couple of times. The other skaters stared at us and got out of the way. Then Scotty set off on his own. That really got people watching. He was so graceful. He went to the middle and did a couple of fancy turns and a spin on one skate. The people standing around the rink started to clap. It was the first time I ever say Scotty so happy.

"You were *won*derful," I said to him. We were in the Rockefeller Center Café having hot chocolate. "Where did you ever learn to skate like that?"

"Oh, I just learned. If I have to join a circus I want to be ready. And ice-skating is great exercise. Right Harrison?"

He was rubbing the seat of his pants and made an exaggerated expression of pain. "How would I know? I did more sitting than skating."

"Wasn't it terrific the way everybody was watching us, and not just because we're a bunch of freaks? I mean they were applauding, and throwing money!"

"They were laughing too," Harrison said. "Especially when Hildy and me skated into that usher and knocked him over the railing."

"It served him right for trying to chase us off the ice," I said. "You have to admit, we were great together. The three of us, a real team, like the three musketeers."

"More like the three *freak*eteers, you mean," Scotty said with a laugh. "When they saw us coming they sure got out of our way in a hurry."

Harrison was thinking. "Wouldn't it be great if we could do that all the time? I mean, if we could form a club, like the WHEELS, and people would stay out of our way? Wouldn't that be something?"

It was like a little light bulb lit up over Scotty's head. "Why don't we do just that?" He licked his marshmallow mustache. His face was glowing, some from the cold, and some from what he was thinking. "We could form a club, and maybe we could even get jackets with names on them, and-"

"And the WHEELS would murder us," Harrison said. "You know they're the *only* club in Vanderville. Carmine Galante made that very clear when he started the WHEELS."

"Well, maybe it's time for that to change." Scotty looked at me, and I looked at Harrison.

"Well-" he said finally, "if you're really sure about this, maybe my mom can help us out. She works in a department store, and I know she can get us the jackets at a discount."

"We'll have to think of a good name for the club," I said.

"That's easy. What's the only thing we could call ourselves?" Scotty asked.

We looked around the table and burst out laughing. "FREAKS!" we yelled together. The rest of the people in the café turned around to stare at us.

Scotty raised his hot chocolate. "A toast," he proposed, "to the three of us. To the FREAKS."

And that was the way it happened.

# Chapter Nine
## "Meet The FREAKs"

It took a couple of weeks before the jackets were ready. At first Harrison's mother didn't think it was such a great idea. She said she wasn't going to get any jackets, and she sure didn't want any son of hers walking around town with the word FREAKS on his back. But Harrison was finally able to convince her that it was a joke. So even though she didn't see the humor of it, she finally agreed to put in the order and Harrison made all of the arrangements.

It was during Christmas vacation that they arrived. Scotty got a brand new ten speed bike from his parents, so when Harrison called him and said that the jackets were in, he tore over to Harrison's house, even though the streets were patched over with snow and ice. Then the two of them raced to my house with the package. They hadn't bothered to open it. They were both out of breath when they arrived.

"Here they are," Harrison announced. He dropped the brown paper bundle on the couch and pulled apart the cord. Three blue satin jackets tumbled out. "Our names are on the front, see."

"They are beautiful!" I held mine up and laughed. "Hildy" was stitched on the left side in script.

"And FREAKS is printed on the back in three inch black letters. I thought black and blue would be appropriate colors for us." He turned his over. "Oh oh!"

"What's the matter?" I looked at the back of mine and Scotty looked at his. The three jackets were the same. All of the letters were three inches except for the "s." That was only one inch.

Harrison was steamed. "I told my mother-"

"It doesn't matter," Scotty said. "They're great just the way they are. And it's kind of poetic too, when you think about it. A little imperfection, just like us."

I slipped my jacket on and turned to see how I looked in the mirror. "I guess that makes us capital f capital r capital e capital a capital k small s," I said and laughed.

That made Harrison feel a little better about things. He and Scotty put theirs on too.

"Aren't we a sight? I can't wait to wear this to school," Scotty said. "And I can't wait to see the look on Carmine Galante's face."

"I can," Harrison said. "I still think the *capital* W-H-E-E-L-S are going to kill us!"

We linked arms and the three of us paraded around the living room.

* * *

I don't think we really expected the stir we made. We had agreed to meet in the locker corridor early the morning school reopened after the New Year. The day was a dreary one, with frozen drops of rain that stuck on the windshield of Daddy's car like button candy. He dropped me off at school on his way to work. When we got there, the teachers' parking lot was empty, the building was dark, and it still wasn't light out.

"Are you *sure*, Hildy, you were supposed to meet the boys so early?" he asked. He wasn't quite certain how he felt about my jacket. I could tell by the look on his face when I tried it on for him. But one thing about my father, he does have an appreciation for the absurd. He told me if wearing a jacket with FREAKs on my back was going to make me happy, he wasn't going to object.

"I'm sure, Daddy," I said. "They must be inside already." I kissed him and ran for the building.

Most of the doors were locked. I found one open on the far side of the building. Inside the corridors were dark and shining clean. The tile floors smelled of wax and pine cleaner. It looked nice without all the junk the kids dumped in the halls. When I found my locker I had some trouble getting the lock open because I couldn't remember my combination.

"Hildy!" I heard Scotty call from out of the darkness. He was coming down the hall leading Harrison. Harrison was all wrapped up in his hat and scarf, like some mummy that escaped from a horror film. His glasses were steamed over so he couldn't see. Neither of them was wearing the jackets.

"Do you have them?" I asked.

Scotty's jacket was in a plastic bag. "I didn't want to get it wet."

Harrison had his on *under* his regular coat. "My mother wouldn't let me out of the house until I covered it up," he explained. "So what's the plan?"

"Well, if we really want to make a big impression, we should wait until everybody's here before we make our entrance." I also figured there was strength in numbers. We didn't know what the WHEELS would do when they got a look at out jackets. "If we could find someplace to hang out until the bell rings, so we won't be seen—"

Scotty thought for a second. "I know just the place, The Pit. First let's put all of our stuff in your locker, Hildy. Then follow me. This is going to be great!"

Scotty led the way down the dark corridor, into the annex and past the Custodian's Office. It was where I first spoke to him the on day of the incident in the cafeteria. It was still a part of the building that I wasn't familiar with. We followed him around some cartons to a door in one of the shadowy recesses. Anybody who didn't know the door was there would have missed it.

"Here it is," Scotty said. "This leads to the main boiler room, I think. But nobody ever uses it hardly, and Mr. Polakas, the custodian, stores stuff here." He turned the knob, but it was locked. "No problem. I know how to open it." He fiddled with the knob and the door opened. He felt along the wall for the light switch.

The room was part of the basement of the annex, down five steps. It reminded me of a dungeon. There were cartons everywhere, and broken desks, some old duplicating machines, cans of duplicating fluid and a bunch of other stuff. They were the relics of another time at Vanderville.

"Welcome to The Pit," Scotty said proudly. "It's one of my recent discoveries, my home away from home. I sometimes use it when I want to get away from everything. It's kind of a sanctuary."

"It's kind of dusty," Harrison said and he started to sneeze.

"It's perfect." I sat on the end of one of the cartons and the three of us waited for the first bell to ring.

It was funny, the reactions of the other kids when we came down the hall. At first there weren't any. It was like the three of us were invisible, among all those kids showing off their new Christmas jewelry, their sweaters and shirts and things. But then, when we passed and they got a good look at the back of our jackets, it was like one of those old cowboy movies. Suddenly the hall got very quiet. I guess the kids were trying to figure out if it was a joke. And then somebody laughed, and then there were a couple of comments. Scotty, Harrison and I just kept right on walking with our arms linked together. Then, all at once, the kids were all over us. They were all saying how cool the jackets were, and what a great idea it was.

Mr. Goldstein heard the racket and came running down the hall yelling. I guess he thought there was a fight going on.

"All right, break it up! Move along! Get to Homeroom!"

Boy, was he surprised when he pushed his way into the middle of things and came face to face with the three FREAKs.

# Chapter Ten
# "Going Underground"

We made official contact with the WHEELS a couple of days later.

I was on the third floor trying to open the elevator door with my key. I was on my way down from the Science Lab. The first week back at school from vacation was my week to stay after and help Mrs. Marshall set up the science experiments for the lab class for the next day. It was her way of giving kids who wanted it a chance to earn extra credit. By the time I was finished arranging all the slides in the microscopes and putting out the displays, the building was deserted. Everyone had escaped into the winter gloom the first chance they got. Harrison and Scotty were home already. They took the regular bus. I looked at the new wristwatch my father had bought me for Christmas. I had just enough time to get to my locker, pick up my books, and catch the late bus. My first week in the FREAKs had been an interesting experience. More kids said hello and smiled at me than *ever* in my whole life. And Mrs. Turnbull made us, or rather us wearing our jackets, into a writing lesson in English class. It was an exercise on labeling and stereotyping, judging people by the way they looked or dressed, instead of by they way they acted. I felt kind of like a celebrity.

It's funny how it worked. All of my life I fought *not* to be considered a freak, and practically nobody knew I was alive. I put on a silly satin jacket with the word FREAKs on the back, and suddenly I was getting noticed.

Of course not everybody was delighted about things. The WHEELS were not too happy, kind of the way we expected. The word got around that the WHEELS was still the only club in school, and that was the way it was going to stay. It was a warning to anybody who had ideas about starting another club, and to the three of us FREAKs in particular.

When I stepped into the elevator Carmine Galante was standing inside. I was really scared and I guess it showed on my face. He reached across me before I could move and he shut the elevator door and pushed the emergency stop button. Everything was so quiet.

"Hello, sweetums. I've been waiting for you."

"Wh-What do you want?" I stuttered. I could hear my voice going way up the way it does whenever I get nervous. I tried to control it.

"Just a little elevator ride with one of my favorite freaks."

"Well, you don't belong in this elevator. It's only for kids who have special passes." I sounded pretty lame, I know, like a real jerk, but it was the only thing I could think to say. It didn't even occur to me to yell or anything. He hadn't touched me. Besides, there probably wasn't anybody who would have heard me anyway.

"This is my pass," he said, showing me the back of his jacket. "That's a pretty jacket you have on." He ran his fingers lightly over the front of it. "And it's just the right name too." All the time he was talking his face had a smile on it that wasn't a smile at all. "I think you like to play games, sweetums. You, that faggot Jew and the shrimp. But you're playing my game now, and I don't lose. This is my school, mine and the WHEELS, and we don't want another club at Vanderville. Is that clear?"

I don't know how I did it, I was so scared that my knees were practically shaking, but I answered him back. "You sound like the dialogue from a bad cowboy movie, 'This town ain't big enough for the both of us.' Well, Vanderville is *our* school too. And the FREAKs are here to stay! Get used to it and now get out of my way." I tried to push past him to get at the "Start" button.

His face changed. "Listen to me, you crooked leg little gimp. I'm not fooling around. Get rid of those jackets before you get something more than you bargained for."

My voice got very calm. "You really must be insecure, Carmine. Have you ever considered talking to a psychiatrist?"

He balled his hands into fists, and for a second I thought he was going to punch me. But he put his face up real close to mine.

"Just in case you don't hear so good, gimp, read my lips. If you think this place is trouble now, wait and see how much worse it can get for you and your friends." He opened the door. Before he slipped out into the hall he reached in and pulled my key out of the panel and dropped it inside the car. Then he turned off the lights. The door closed and everything was pitch dark. "Have a nice ride, sweetums," he called through the closed door.

It was awful. First I felt around the floor with my foot, but I couldn't find the key. Then I think I panicked, and I started to cry. The next thing, I was crawling around the bottom of the elevator on my hands and knees. I could feel the tears rolling down my cheeks.

"Are you still here, Hildy?" Mrs. Marshall asked when I finally got down to the first floor. She was coming out of the Main Office with her things. "I'm sure you missed the late bus. I hope you have a ride home. It's pouring out." Then she looked at my face. "Hildy dear, are you all right? What happened to you?"

"I'm all right, Mrs. Marshall. I just got stuck in the elevator."

Mrs. Marshall drove me home.

* * *

"He didn't hurt you, did he?" Scotty asked. He was on the extension at Harrison's house. I had called Harrison as soon as Mrs. Marshall dropped me off.

"No, he didn't hurt me, but he could have if he wanted to. He sure scared me though. And he was real steamed about our jackets." I repeated what Carmine had said and what I had told him in the elevator.

"What are we going to do?" Harrison asked. "Do we dump the jackets?"

Nobody said anything.

"We knew what the reaction was going to be," Scotty said, "and we decided to get them anyway."

"The WHEELS picked on us *before* we got our jackets," Harrison said.

"That's right, and even if we get rid of them, you don't think things are going to change, do you? We antagonize them just because we're alive. The question is, do we want to antagonize them more than we usually do?"

"They're bigger than we are," Harrison offered.

"But we're *smarter*," Scotty said. "You said it yourself. If we put our heads together I'm sure we can beat them. What do you say? Are we *FREAKs* or are we *wimps*?"

"Personally," Harrison said, "*I'm* a wimp. But I'll go along with whatever the two of you decide."

I was silent. I was still shaking from the elevator.

"I have an idea," Scotty said after a minute. "I know how the WHEELS operate. Think for a minute. What's the tactic they rely on most?"

"Fear," I answered.

"As far as tactics go," Harrison said, "it sure works with me. Whenever I see them coming down the halls I want to run and hide."

"That's *exactly* what they count on. You notice they never pick on groups. They keep people in line one at a time. They haven't even come after *us* when we're together. They wait until we're separated, isolated. Like Carmine did with Hildy. And then they pounce. Most of the stunts they pull are sneaky things, to annoy a person, to frighten, to wear him down. "Like-"

"Like changing a lock on a locker," I said.

"Exactly," Scotty replied.

"Or like when they filled my locker with Jello and with dog poop. Or when they smeared paper paste on all my lab reports because I wouldn't let Lester Cooper copy them."

"See how it works? One at a time. Chip, chip, chip. Like a little hammer on a big rock."

"But what can we do?" I asked. "We can't walk around like Siamese triplets all day. We can't stay together *all* the time."

"Of course not. But if we want to stay FREAKs, we'll have to anticipate them. Out-think them. Be ready for them. We'll have to eliminate the things we *know* the WHEELS are going to hit."

"The lockers!" Harrison said, beginning to follow Scotty's idea.

"Right, our lockers. And our lab folders in the Science Lab. And our art projects. Anything they can get their hands on."

"So?"

"So Monday we get to school real early and clean everything out."

"But where will we put it all? Our books and coats and stuff?"

"In The Pit. It's the perfect place. Nobody knows about it but us. We can leave everything there. And when we aren't in class, we can go there and hide out!"

"And the rest of the time?"

"The rest of the time we'll be real careful out there. Besides, we'll be together, or with teachers. And who knows, once the WHEELS can't find us, and can't do anything to *our* lockers, we might be able to give *them* a dose of their own medicine. The FREAKs are going *underground*!"

My father came in as I hung up the phone. "What's up?" he asked. "You look serious."

"Just making plans to go underground," I answered.

* * *

So we went underground.

Monday morning I got up real early. I made a pot of coffee for my father and left him a note saying that I had to do something before school started. I didn't want to worry him. Harrison and Scotty swung past my house on their bikes and rode me to school on the handlebars.

I cleaned out my locker of everything and put the lock back on. Then I carried all of my stuff to where they were waiting.

"Did you move out of your house?" I asked when I saw everything that Harrison was carrying. He was overloaded with papers, books, a complete change of clothes and *two* umbrellas.

"'Be prepared,' I always say."

"Is that all of it?" Scotty asked.

"Except for our lab experiments and art projects. The classrooms were locked."

"I think the most important thing is the lockers. We can pick up the other stuff during the day. We don't know when they'll hit, but at least we got a head start on them.

This'll help too." Scotty pulled a little tube out of his pocket. "*Crazy Glue*. A couple of drops in each of their locks and that'll keep them busy for a while. Wait for me, I'll be right back."

When Scotty got back, and before anybody else came in, we sneaked off to The Pit and settled in. It wasn't bad at all. There was a folding card table, some chairs, and even an old radio.

The plan was simple, stay away from the WHEELS and keep together as much as possible. We agreed to meet back at The Pit during lunch and study hall and at the end of the day. Since Harrison was an unofficial aide, he could run all over the building without being challenged. And because Scotty had a reputation for being rowdy, most of the teachers were only too glad to get rid of him when Harrison came to get him for the dean or something. And it was easy for me to get a pass from any of my teachers. All I had to do was tell them that I had to go to the nurse. Because I was on the "Confidential List" all the teachers had, they never questioned me. Not that I did that kind of stuff very often.

I made sure to stay clear of the elevator and the girl's room. I didn't want to get cut off again. And although I saw the WHEELS a couple of times during the day from afar, we managed to avoid each other, like ships passing in a fog. Harrison and Scotty were just as lucky. At the end of the day we met in The Pit and walked out together.

"I checked my locker," Scotty said, "and there wasn't anything unusual. I wonder how *they* did with *their* lockers."

"It was a wonderful day," Harrison said. "I moved like a shadow through the halls." He ducked and he tiptoed and ducked again. "In and out of class. I guess I was too smooth and slick for them. I didn't see the WHEELS all day."

"Yeah," Scotty said. "We were slick all right. We thought of everything, everything except *one* thing. Look!"

"The *bikes*!" Harrison groaned.

We ran up to the two piles of metal that used to be Harrison's homemade bike and Scotty's new ten-speed. The tires were flat. The rims were bent and the frames twisted beyond repair.

"It looks like we're at war," Scotty cried.

# Chapter Eleven
## "Hop-Frog"

The war raged on for another week.

The three of us continued to wear our jackets every day to all of our classes. The rest of the time we were underground and out of sight. But not out of mind. The WHEELS were hot on our trail. Harrison's locker was trashed, and a stink bomb dumped inside. For two days the locker corridor smelled like a science experiment involving rotten eggs and sulfa. Then Scotty's locker was spray painted, inside and out. I knew that I was next.

I was in English class with Harrison when we heard the explosion. Mrs. Turnbull was in the middle of an Emily Dickinson poem, showing us how pretty nearly all of her poetry can be sung to the tune "The Yellow Rose of Texas." It was interesting, and even the kids who didn't like poetry were paying attention.

"My goodness!" she said. "What was that?" She opened the classroom door and looked out into the corridor. The smell of gunpowder drifted into the room.

Harrison leaned over to me and whispered, "I'll bet you whatever you have for lunch today it was your locker."

Then the fire alarm went off. Mrs. Turnbull lined us up and we followed her along the emergency escape route to the outside of the building. It was nasty and cold, and practically the whole school was huddled together shivering and trying to keep warm. But we had to wait outside until the fire department arrived and allowed us back in.

It wasn't long before the P.A. speaker snapped and crackled as Mr. Fagan took to the airwaves. He blew into the microphone the way he always did before he talked.

"This is Mr. Fagan speaking. Stop all work. Stop all work." That was what he always said. He pounded the microphone with his fingers a couple of times and blew into it some more. Then he gave a seven and a half minute lecture about how the school belonged to everybody, and how we were all part of the "school family." He said that some vandals were attacking the security of that family and these acts of "wanton destruction of community property" had better stop.

He went on and on, using the metaphor of the family. He said that as the principal of the school, he was like the father. "There are some youngsters–" That was Mr. Fagan's way of referring to junior high school kids. He never said kids, and he couldn't call us children. "–who are misbehaving," he said, "and if this situation isn't remedied immediately, I will be forced to take stern measures. What I mean is, unless the vandalism stops, the innocent along with the guilty will have to suffer the consequences. Now I know that you may be thinking that isn't fair, and I realize that the greater majority of you are not to blame, but the wheat can not always be separated from the chaff-"

I kind of got the feeling that Mr. Fagan was more concerned about *how* he sounded when he talked instead of worrying about *what* he was saying. He always seemed to start off okay, but by the time he got to the second or third sentence, he was so caught up in things that nobody could follow what he meant. Nobody was listening anyway. I even saw Mrs. Turnbull looking over some of her notes while he continued.

Only once in the time I was in Vanderville do I remember a lecture that Mr. Fagan gave that was right to the point. It was during a snowstorm. He came on the P.A. and announced that the snow was good for making snowballs, and then he warned us of the dangers of throwing snowballs at people and passing cars. He was particularly concerned about ice balls that could smash a car or school bus windshield quite easily. And he said under no circumstances should youngsters put rocks or other foreign matter into their snowballs. After that speech more kids went out and threw stuff at the school buses than if he hadn't said anything at all.

Anyway, he finished talking about vandalism just as the bell rang. He threatened to cancel the approaching Ninth Grade Dance unless the mischief stopped. But I don't think anybody heard him. They were out screaming in the halls going to their next classes.

Harrison was right about my locker. We passed it on the way to The Pit. Someone had put an M-80 firecracker in the door and practically blew the whole thing off the hinges. Luckily it was empty and no damage was done, to any of my stuff, I mean.

But it looked like the rest of the school was caught up in the middle of our war, and *they* were suffering the consequences.

* * *

Later that day Scotty came bursting into The Pit. His face was as red as fire and his eyes were bugging out. He was so out of breath he could hardly talk.

"H-Hildy! H-Harrison!"

"What is it? What's the matter?" We thought he was being chased. "Is it the WHEELS?"

He shook his head and held up a book. Harrison took it from him and showed me the title. It was the *Complete Tales and Poems of Edgar Allan Poe*. The cover of the book had the title spelled out in black and yellow and orange to resemble a skull.

"Yeah?" Harrison said.

"Yeah!" Scotty replied when he could talk. "This is only *the* best book ever written in the whole world! When Masher saw me in the hall, I ducked into the school library to get away from him. He wouldn't be caught dead in any place that has books and where people can read. I found this in the library. Or I should say that *it* found *me*. I was ducking behind a shelf and the book fell out all by itself and practically hit me on the head. It was like magic. Turn to page five hundred and two."

Harrison opened the book and it went right to the page. "'Hop-Frog'?"

"That's it! That's the story! When the book fell it opened to that exact page, like somebody was sending me a message. I already read it three times." He pulled the book out of Harrison's hands. "It's a little hard to understand because the vocabulary is difficult and the sentences are long and involved. But it's worth the effort, believe me. It's about Hop-Frog, only that isn't his real name. And he's a dwarf! A court jester. A fool they called him. And listen to this, Hildy. He's a cripple too! You have to read it, the both of you. It's great the way he gets even with this evil king and his men for hurting his girlfriend. She's a dwarf too! Let me read it to you." He started. "No, it'll take too long, so I'll just tell you all about it and you can read it later."

So for the next ten minutes Scotty told us the story in every detail.

It was about this king and his seven ministers who lived somewhere in Europe a long time ago. They were all big and fat, and cruel, especially to the dwarf, Hop-Frog. He had been kidnapped from his home in the jungles or something, and brought to the court along with Trippetta, his girlfriend, who was also a dwarf, but perfect in proportion, and very beautiful.

The king loved to play practical jokes on everybody, and he didn't care who got hurt. He especially made fun of Hop-Frog, and gave him that name because he couldn't walk, and he kind of wiggled and hopped like a frog when he moved. But Hop-Frog had strong arms and a big chest, and he could climb trees and ropes and things without any trouble at all.

One day the king announced that there was going to be a giant costume party for his entire court, a masquerade. He got Hop-Frog and Trippetta to make all the arrangements. Everybody who was going to the party had already decided on a costume. Everybody but the king and his ministers. On the night of the party they still hadn't decided, so the king called Hop-Frog and Trippetta and told them to come up with something fast. Then he forced Hop-Frog to drink wine, even though the king knew that wine made Hop-Frog very sad, and a little bit crazy. And when Trippetta tried to stop the king, he slapped her and threw a drink in her face. That was when Hop-Frog came up with the idea for a costume.

He called it the "Eight Chained Orangutans," and he said it was very popular in his country, and that it would be a terrific joke that would probably scare everybody at the party. The plan was to dress up the king and his ministers to look like apes, and chain them together. On the stroke of midnight they would all come running into the hall like they escaped from a zoo or something. That sounded like a great idea to the king, so he let Hop-Frog smear tar all over them and then stick this furry stuff on top of the tar. He told them to wait for just the right moment before they appeared, and then Hop-Frog went into the hall to make some final arrangements.

On the second of midnight, as the clock was striking twelve, they all came tumbling in, scaring everybody to death almost. Hop-Frog moved them to the center of the hall, before anybody realized who they were, or what was happening. And then he attached another chain, the one that was used to hold a giant chandelier, right onto the king and his men.  He gave a signal and the chain went up slowly, lifting the eight of them into the air.

That was when Hop-Frog grabbed a torch and jumped over them, yelling and screaming what evil men they all were.  And he set them on fire with the torch and climbed up the chain and escaped.

"Let me read the last part to you," Scotty said.  He opened the book and read the last paragraph.  "'The eight corpses swung in their chains, a fetid, blackened, hideous and indistinguishable mass. The cripple hurled his torch at them, clambered leisurely to the ceiling, and disappeared through the skylight.  It is supposed that Trippetta, stationed on the roof of the salon, had been the accomplice of her friend in his fiery revenge, and that, together, they effected their escape to their own country; for neither was seen again.'"

The whole time Scotty was telling the story it was as though he wasn't in The Pit with us, but there, with Trippetta and Hop-Frog.  It was almost like Scotty had become Hop-Frog.

"Gross!" Harrison said when he was finished.

"Great!" Scotty said.  "He really got even with them.  He taught all of them a lesson all right."  Scotty jumped on one of the cartons and kicked his legs.  Then he was up again, climbing over the boxes and laughing.  "I never read a story before where the hero was a dwarf.  That Poe really knows what it's like.  I wonder if he's a dwarf?"  He was balancing on the metal shelf way over our heads, looking down on Harrison and me.

"He wasn't," I said.  I had done a report on Poe in one of my other schools.  "But he knew what it was like to suffer because he led a very tragic life.  He was an orphan. His adopted father threw him out of the house.  He even got expelled from West Point. He married his cousin, Virginia, when she was only fourteen.  She was the only person he ever truly loved, but she died and something snapped in Poe.  He kind of committed suicide when he stopped caring for himself and he was only forty when he died."

"He's *dead*?" Scotty asked.  He climbed down from the shelf.  "I just found him, and he's dead?"

"For a long time," Harrison said.  "Don't you remember we studied him in eighth grade?"

"I never paid any attention to that stuff."  Scotty looked really sad.

"He wrote poetry too. 'Annabel Lee' and 'The Raven' are about his dead wife." I thumbed through the book. "They're in here too." And there was a biography in the back of the book. "He's been dead for more than a hundred years. He died in 1849."

"Brother," Scotty said.

I knew exactly how felt. It was like the time I saw this old movie with this actor Robert Walker, and I fell in love. Then I found out he was already dead. And the same thing happened with another actor named John Garfield. For a while it seemed like *everybody* I loved was already dead. So I understood how Scotty felt.

"Well," Scotty said, "it doesn't matter that he's dead. I'm going to read every story and poem in this book. And this is still the greatest story ever written. I don't know how he did it, but it's like Poe wanted *me* to find this book. It's like he knew about *my* life. 'Hop-Frog' is a story about *all of us*. It's about the FREAKs. Only he gets even." He went and sat on the steps. "Don't you ever wonder why this joke was played on us? I mean, in the plan for the whole universe, why was it so important that I be a dwarf, or you a cripple, or Harrison end up with a rheumatic heart? Who decided it? Who made up the rules?"

"It'll make you crazy to think about stuff like that. Things are just the way they are, and you can't do anything to change them," Harrison said. "There are a lot of people who are a lot worse off."

"That's what my family always says. And there are a lot of people a lot better off than us. But I'm tired of it. I don't want to play by these rules any more. Think about it, about your life, and where you're going to be ten years from now, or twenty. What are you going to be? What's your life going to be like? Then picture your wildest dream come true, your greatest fantasy, and what it would be like if you were born normal and could do anything."

"We all think like that, I guess," I said.

"Well, what would *you* be, Hildy?"

"A dancer," I said without hesitation. "Classical ballet, just like my mother. And I'd tour the country, the world, dancing 'Swan Lake.' A command performance in the White House at Christmas. That was always my dream."

Harrison said, "I think I'd be a great baseball player, and I'd hit a homerun in the last game of the World Series and be a hero. Then all those kids who never picked me for their teams in gym would be sorry." He thought about it. "Nah! Too trivial. I'd be a scientist and cure something."

"What about you, Scotty?" I asked. "What's your fantasy?"

"To be *five feet tall*!" he said. He was serious. "You know, in my house, my mother and father used to mark a place on the door molding when me and my brothers and sister were growing up. They made little nicks in the paint and marked them with our names and the date and stuff. They stopped doing that with me when I was five years old and I stopped growing. Every time I pass the place in the kitchen I look at the marks, and where mine leave off. Even now, I still do it. All I *ever* wanted to be was five feet tall. And I'm never going to be."

"So," I said, "I'll *never* be a dancer. And Harrison will never hit a homerun in the World Series. That doesn't matter much. We'll do other things with our lives. You *can* be a writer and write about what you think and feel, so that other people can understand. Just like Poe did."

"Still, it's not fair, Hildy. No matter what you say, *it's just not fair*!"

"Life's not fair," Harrison said. "My mother tells me that *all the time*. She's always saying to my father how she could have married her first boyfriend and been rich and driving a Mercedes and living in Florida right now. And my father says he wishes she had."

Scotty and I laughed.

"But still, it sure would be great if we could get even, just a little. Like Hop-Frog did."

"And maybe get the WHEELS to dress up like monkeys and set them on fire? Gross!"

"Maybe not that, exactly. But we could mess around with *their* stuff for a change." Scotty's face was a sly grin. "We owe them for what they did to our bikes. For what Carmine did to Hildy in the elevator."

"I don't know," I said. "You heard Mr. Fagan's announcement. He said *all* the vandalism has to stop or he'll cancel the Ninth Grade Dance."

"So?" Scotty said. "I don't know about you, but *I* wasn't planning to go. Besides, no one would ever figure it was us." Scotty smacked the book. "What do you say? It's about time we tipped the scales of justice a little."

I looked at Harrison.

He pushed his glasses up on his nose and made a face. "But let's *not* set them on fire, okay?"

# Chapter Twelve
## "Using Your Head"

It was meant to be a joke, on the WHEELS, a "grand jest" in the style of "Hop-Frog." At least that was what we intended. But before it was over, there weren't too many people, including Mr. Fagan, who were laughing.

Scotty had sent a message for Harrison and me. We usually got word to each other by writing coded notes on a desk in Mrs. Turnbull's class. Or we left them on slips of paper stuck under the water fountain across from the Guidance Center. Harrison made up the code and we memorized it. It was really kind of simple, and anybody who wanted to take the time could figure it out eventually. The vowels, including Y, were the numbers backwards from six to one, and the remaining letters were backwards from Z. It probably wasn't necessary, but we had fun with the code anyway.

"Q55K=Q5=4P=KU5=O4K=6WK5M=LYU33R=K3X61=Z5=OM5O6M5X=K3 =LK61= R6K5-L," the message said. "Meet me in The Pit after school today-be prepared to stay late-S."

When Harrison and I got there, Scotty was sitting at the table looking real smug, kind of like the cat that swallowed the canary.

"What's up?" Harrison asked. "Your message sounded really important."

Scotty raised his eyebrows a couple of times and smiled. "You'll never guess what I have here." He pulled a plastic garbage bag from under the table and uncovered a small package about the size of a volleyball. It was wrapped in brown paper that was stained darker in places.

"What *is* that mess?" I asked.

"A head," he said, and delicately unwrapped the contents of the soggy paper.

"A *head*? Whose? You're kidding, I hope." I was really grossed out by the thought.

He held up what turned out to be the poor remains of an animal. Its eyes were opened wide. Its tongue stuck out from its mouth. It had been skinned and pieces of meat were where its cheeks used to be.

"That's disgusting," I managed without gagging.

"It's neat," Harrison said with the detachment of a scientist. He gave the head a closer inspection. "Sheep?"

"A lamb's head. I got it from my cousin. He's a butcher. I told him I needed it for a school project."

"Is it for Biology Lab?" Harrison asked hopefully. He could hardly wait to get a good look at what was inside the poor thing.

"No, not exactly." Scotty couldn't control a giggle. "It's for Carmine Galante and the WHEELS. Can you imagine what he'll do on Monday when he opens his locker and comes face to face with this beauty?" He broke into a laugh, and Harrison and I couldn't help laughing too, when we pictured it.

We waited until the building was empty before we left The Pit. Scotty carried the head all wrapped in the bag, and we sneaked carefully down the hall. Harrison and I were the lookouts while Scotty found Carmine Galante's locker. He tried several combinations but they didn't work.

"I *never* did anything like *this* before," Harrison whispered nervously. "It's always me that's being trashed."

"Isn't it nice to be on the other side for a change?" Scotty asked.

"I just hope nobody catches us. My mother will kill me if-"

"Shhh!" Scotty said. His ear was pressed against the lock while his fingers turned another combination. "Got it!" The lock clicked and snapped open.

The inside of the locker was a mess. It was full of things, pictures of girls in bikinis, rock groups and stuff like that. "WHEELS Headquarters" was written in black magic marker on the door, and "Death Before Dishonor" was under that. There were a bunch of drawings of knives dripping blood, coiled snakes, and a skull and cross bones with lightening bolts poking through the eye sockets.

"With everything else that's in here, he may not even notice that lamb's head," Harrison said.

Scotty unwrapped the package. "Don't worry, by Monday morning he'll notice it. Quick," he handed me the head, "put it on the shelf. I can't reach."

"Hurry up, I think somebody's coming!" Harrison said.

I really didn't want to touch it, but I propped it on the shelf. It made me feel funny inside.

"Turn it around so the face is pointing out."

My hands were all slimy, but I did what he said.

"Let's get out of here. Mr. Polakas is coming!" Harrison started to run and we followed.

"I can't wait until Monday," Scotty said.

I couldn't wait to get home and wash my hands.

* * *

I was in history class with Mr. Cheslak, finishing the last of the Crusades, when the door opened and the Hall Patrol arrived. Mr. Cheslak kept right on going, reading from the textbook just like he hadn't noticed. The whole time he was making his way slowly toward the door. When he got there he did a quick spin around and made the kid who was standing there jump.

"Mr. O'Brien," Mr. Cheslak hissed through his teeth.

Mr. Cheslak always called kids "mister" or "miss," and never by their first name. Sometimes when he called on us in class he called us "knaves" or "varlets" or "rogues" and medieval stuff like that. But he didn't mean anything bad by it. There was always a kind of smile on his face, and by the tone of his voice, we knew that Mr. Cheslak really liked kids.

"To what do we owe the honor of your little intrusion into the wonderful world of history, the Kingdom of Cheslakia?"

The kid's face got real red.

"Enter, varlet, and state your business quickly and be gone!" He picked up the map pointer and whipped it in front of him like a dueling foil. The class laughed and O'Brien flinched.

He came completely into the room. He was a Ninth Grader, wearing a Hall Patrol Captain's badge and armband. At Vanderville the Hall Patrol helped move the human traffic in the halls during the passing of classes. They ran errands and rounded up the kids who had to go to detention after school.

"M-Mr. Cheslak-" he started.

"Yes, that has been established. I *am* Mr. Cheslak. And you are, no doubt, the Captain of the Guard in quest of some blackguard to cast into the dungeon."

"No, sir. I-I mean, yes, sir. I mean-"

Mr. Cheslak always did stuff like that. He said it helped a person to think clearly under normal conditions if they could think under stress. I think he just enjoyed creating a little confusion and playing jokes on people. Once he got the whole class to jump up and sing every time somebody came into the classroom. He told us to sing even if it was the principal or the superintendent of schools who walked in. It was a silly song that went, "Whosoever invades the privacy of this room, is tempting fate and risking doom." But it was fun, and we all did it.

Now the class was really laughing at poor O'Brien.

"'No, I mean yes'?" he pressed. "In the name of the Holy Roman Emperor, make up your mind, lad. What is it, Captain? Speak up, man, before I have your head served up on a platter." He made a lunge with his pointer-sword.

The boy started again, real fast. "Mr. Fagan would like to see Hilda Crocket in the Main Office right now! Please," he added.

Every head in the room turned to me. Every eye stared at me. I could feel the inside of my stomach cave in.

"Miss Crocket?" Mr. Cheslak raised one eyebrow. "Are you sure?" He turned his attention to me. "And just what kind of impish devilment have you been up to now, wench?"

"I don't know, Mr. Cheslak." That's what I said, but I had a pretty good idea. I packed my books together and when I walked to the door I could feel everybody in class watching me.

Out in the hall Harrison was leaning against the wall. His head was down and his hands were clasped in front of him, like he was wearing handcuffs. He looked worse than I felt.

"Hildy," he said when he saw me, "we are in *deep* trouble. I mean, like a capital offense. Our heads are on the block and the ax is about to fall!"

"What happened to your neck?" I asked. There were red marks all over it.

He pushed his glasses up on his nose. "Nothing compared to what my mother will do when she finds out what happened. She's going to murder me. What's *left* of me."

"Tell me what happened."

On the trip to the office Harrison told me the whole story while O'Brien stayed close to hear.

That morning Scotty convinced Harrison to go with him and watch what was going to happen. Scotty didn't just want to scare Carmine, he wanted to see it. They were hiding in the locker corridor waiting. According to Harrison that lamb's head was really ripe! They could smell it all the way down the hall. When Carmine got within yards of his locker he started sniffing. He knew there was something in there, but he wasn't prepared for what he saw when he opened the door. Harrison said Carmine jumped two feet in the air, straight up, when he came eyeball to eyeball with that head.

"And he screamed! Carmine Galante actually screamed! And he tried to run away. It was just like in the cartoons, Hildy," Harrison said. "His legs were moving, but he wasn't going anywhere. And the whole time he was making this moaning sound like he was going to die. You should've seen it. It was so funny."

"I'm sorry I missed it," I said, and I was.

"But there's more. Scotty and I started to laugh. I mean, we cracked up. And Carmine heard us, and then he saw us. Boy, was he mad. Madder than I *ever* saw him get. He went back into the locker and came out with the head in his hands! And he started chasing us, cursing us and calling us names. I never ran so fast in my life. But Scotty kept turning around and running backwards and laughing at him more. And Carmine looked like he was going to explode. All the kids in the hall saw him and they were laughing at him. That was when I tripped and Carmine caught me by the back of my jacket and almost choked me. That's how I got these marks on my neck."

They looked terrible.

"Scotty saved my life though. He came running back, yelling and screaming, and he kicked Carmine right in the seat of his pants. Carmine let me go and ran after him. Right through the cafeteria, over the benches and under the tables, and right into Miss Kesselmeyer's Home Ec class. That's when Carmine threw the head at Scotty. Only it missed Scotty and it landed right on Miss Kesselmeyer's desk. I got there just in time to see it. She let out a scream. There was almost a riot right there in her room, with all the kids in the class running out and yelling. And poor fat Miss Kesselmeyer went down like a ton of bricks."

Miss Kesselmeyer weighed about three hundred pounds. I could picture what it must've been like. "She fainted?" I asked.

"At least I think she fainted. She might have had a heart attack. But Scotty got away, and then Mr. Goldstein came running in and grabbed Carmine and dragged him down to the office. He didn't even *try* to pick Miss Kesselmeyer up."

Harrison finished just as we had reached the Main Office.

"Sit there," the secretary told Harrison and me pointing to the detention chairs that were in the fenced-in area just outside Mr. Fagan's office. Scotty was already there, kicking his feet back and forth, like he always did when he was nervous. When he saw us he smiled.

"Hildy, you should've seen."

"Harrison told me. Are you all right?"

"Sure. I'm just sorry about Miss Kesselmeyer. The custodian wheeled her into the nurse's office on a hand truck."

"Oh, God!" Harrison said. "If Miss Kesselmeyer dies, that makes us murderers!" His face started breaking out with hives and he started to hyperventilate. "Do they have the death penalty in this state? I'm too young to die! I haven't fully reached puberty yet! My mother is really going to kill me."

"It's all right, Harrison." I was trying to calm him down, but I wasn't really sure it *was* all right.

We could hear loud talking through the principal's door.

"That's Mr. Goldstein," Scotty said. "He's in there with Mr. Fagan and Carmine."

"Maybe they'll forget about us," Harrison said hopefully.

"Fat chance," Scotty said, kicking his feet harder. "They're just waiting for the others."

Just then the other two WHEELS arrived in the office, escorted by three more hall guards. They came into the detention area and glared at us. Then Mr. Goldstein opened Mr. Fagan's door and ordered us all inside.

It was the first time I was in Mr. Fagan's office, and it was really pretty nice the way it was decorated. All of the walls were paneled in dark wood and covered with old framed photos of Vanderville throughout the years. There were pictures of kids getting awards and stuff, and the marching band, and a picture of Mr. Fagan when he was young, shaking hands with somebody who was giving him a bowling trophy. The very same trophy, a little tarnished now, was on his desk, along with a picture of Mrs. Fagan, someone who had to be his daughter and his granddaughter. They all looked pretty much alike.

There was a bunch of folding chairs in front of his desk. Carmine Galante was slouching in one of them. His face was kind of pale and his mouth was closed real tight. I could see the place near his temples moving up and down. Mr. Goldstein went to stand behind him and nudged him to sit up straight in his seat.

"Well," Mr. Fagan started. "I guess you know the reason I called this meeting." He had a little smile on his face, but when he saw me limp in, his expression changed and he got real serious.

The two WHEELS looked at each other and at Carmine. His eyes flashed a little and he touched his finger to his lips, to signal them just to keep quiet. Harrison sank down a little in his chair. His face was blotchy.

"We have a serious problem here in Vanderville," Mr. Fagan started again. "Well, that's not to say that other schools on Long Island, or even around the country, for that matter, don't have similar problems. In point of fact, when you compare *our* problem to those of *other* schools around the country, the problems here at Vanderville seem minimal."

It kind of sounded like Mr. Fagan was giving a public relations speech to the PTA. I could tell that he was really winding up for a long one. And so could Mr. Goldstein. He started fidgeting.

"'As the twig is bent, so grows the tree,' the saying goes. Every school has its bent twigs." He looked directly at me. "I'm speaking figuratively now, young lady you understand. What I mean to say is, every school has its few youngsters who are in need of special care and guidance. Here at Vanderville, compared to other schools, that number is probably fewer-"

Mr. Goldstein shuffled his feet and cleared his throat.

Mr. Fagan got the message and his tone changed. "We have had a breach of the peace here. Vandalism, disruption of classes, assaults on students. And this latest incident involving Miss Kesselmeyer. Now I mean to tell you that there are teachers in this school who think the crux of the problem lies with the cliques, the special interest groups, the clubs that have sprung up here in Vanderville. And I have been advised by these same concerned faculty members to take action to break up these cliques." His tone changed again and his voice softened. "I just want you to know that I was once a youngster myself. And when I went to school, back in the Stone Age," he laughed at his little joke, "I belonged to a club too. We called ourselves the 'Peppers,' and we were very active in school events. We organized pep rallies, led the cheers at all the sporting events. We collected toys for orphans at Christmas, and food and clothes for the needy. Of course we didn't wear club jackets, but I'll have you know, I was proud to be a 'Pepper.' All of us 'Peppers' were. We served our community, and we were an important part of the school family. Being a 'Peppers' helped to develop character and strength. So you can see that I understand how a club can be a source of self-identity and self-esteem." Mr. Fagan paused to let his little story sink in.

"But," he continued, "when the aims of a club deviate from the aims of society and the general good, they have to be re-examined. The aims of the club, I mean." He stood up and walked around his desk. He stopped in front of Scotty. "This latest incident is *most* serious because it involves a teacher. You youngsters can't imagine the delicate political position a school principal is in. What with the teachers' union, the PTA, the Board of Education. Just imagine what would happen to me if the School Board heard about things like this. Or the newspapers. All those questions, all those accusations. Imagine having to air all of our dirty linen, so to speak, in public. There are people out there eager to ride any issue like this right into political office. So, I am perfectly within my rights to call your parents. To suspend you. Or even to *expel* you!"

Harrison let out a moan.

"But-" Mr. Fagan let the word hang in the air. "Fortunately Miss Kesselmeyer was not seriously hurt. And she has agreed *not* to press civil charges. So we can keep these events within our school family."

Harrison let out a deep breath and looked around at me and Scotty.

"Of course, I do expect that you will write a letter of apology to Miss Kesselmeyer. Both of you." He indicated Carmine and Scotty. "And in addition, you will be excluded from the Ninth Grade Dance." He stopped and let his words sink in. "As for your respective clubs, because I am sensitive to the positive aspects they can represent, I am *not* going to abolish them from school. But you will have to refrain from wearing your club jackets to or about the school for one month!"

This time it was Mr. Goldstein who moaned.

"Is there something you'd like to add, Mr. Goldstein?" Mr. Fagan asked.

Mr. Goldstein was fuming. He looked directly at the WHEELS. "Almost certainly these hoodlums were the ones who were responsible for the break-in into my office." Scotty turned away and started kicking his feet. "And you're not even going to call their parents? You're going to exclude them from some dance and ban their jackets for a *whole* month? After this latest incident-"

"Mr. Goldstein," Mr. Fagan interrupted, "this is a separate matter. As for the break-in, that was in the past. And you know as well as I, that these youngsters were questioned quite thoroughly by me concerning the matter, to the satisfaction of the police and myself. Now I suggest that you let it remain in the past and try to deal with present matters."

Boy, did Mr. Goldstein's face get red. Carmine Galante's face cracked in a wide smirk that he didn't even try to hide.

"In that case," Mr. Goldstein said, "I have nothing more to say to you, Mr. Fagan. I think you said it *all*." He turned and stormed out of the office and didn't even shut the door.

"Now," Mr. Fagan said when he was gone, "I want you all to shake hands and make friends." He took Carmine and Scotty by the shoulder and made them shake. Then he waited until we all shook hands. "And this is the end of it," he pronounced. "Let's bury the past and any animosities with it. We're one, big, happy family again. Now get on back to your classes, and have a nice day."

But that wasn't the end of it by any stretch. When we got out into the corridor Carmine turned on Scotty. "Don't think it's over, squirt. You and your friends are dead meat!"

"I won't loose any sleep over it, dirt bag!" Scotty snapped back.

They would have started a fight right there, but Mr. Fagan came out of his office just then. He was looking quite content, like he had just solved the Arab-Israeli problem. I really think he believed he might be eligible for the Noble Peace Prize or something and get his picture on the cover of *Time* magazine, Man of the Year, for all his diplomatic work.

"Hurry now," he called, "before you youngsters are late for class."

# Chapter Thirteen
# "Into The Woods"

It sure didn't take long for the news to get around school. Everybody in Vanderville was talking about what Scotty and Harrison had done to Carmine Galante and the WHEELS. They were heroes. And even though I wasn't there, because I was one of the FREAKs, I was sort of a hero too.

It was amazing how many kids seemed to come out of hiding once they realized that the WHEELS were vulnerable. Lots of kids who ignored me the whole time I was in Vanderville started talking to me. And they started doing things for me, like holding doors and stuff. One kid in history class, one of the kids who took a lot from the WHEELS, passed me a Tootsie Roll and a note that said simply, "Thanks."

I was talking about it in The Pit with Harrison and Scotty.

"Today Doreen McFeeley came up to me before Chorus and practically begged me to be her partner for the final duet."

Doreen was the president of Student Council, co-captain of the Kick Line, and vice-president of the Leaders Club. She was the trendsetter in school, always wearing the newest fashions and things *before* anybody else in Vanderville did. She was smart, pretty and conceited. And she had never noticed me before.

Scotty must have read my mind. "Doreen McFeeley is a snob," he said. "Last week she didn't know you were alive. She's just interested in cashing in on your new status. And where were all those other kids the whole year while the WHEELS were making our lives miserable? Just wait until the WHEELS regroup and come after us. When the chips are down, everybody will disappear again, just as fast."

"Do you think they really will come after us?" It was a silly question. Carmine Galante said it wasn't over.

"You better believe it," Scotty said. "It's just a matter of where and when."

For that reason we had decided to stay in The Pit later than usual, to give everybody in the building, including the WHEELS, a chance to get home. And instead of taking the late bus, we thought we'd sneak home on foot. We figured it would be wise to vary our routine and make it tougher on the WHEELS, in case they were watching.

Outside everybody was gone except for Duncan Dumont and his cousin, Ali. They were sitting by the bike racks over near the basketball courts. I had seen the two of them around school before, but I really didn't know them, and I hadn't talked to them. They had moved to Vanderville just before I did, from South Carolina or someplace. The two of them stayed together all of the time because not many of the other kids had much to do with them. They were the only two black kids in the whole school. They watched as we cut across the track toward the woods behind the school.

Just on the other side of the ball field there was a wooded area. Not a real forest or anything, just a bunch of trees that hadn't been cut down yet to build houses or a strip mall. There were pine trees and some spruce that made the woods smell like Christmas all the time. Kids on dirt bikes sometimes rode on the dirt trails between the trees. At night they hung out there and drank beer and stuff. The place was littered with cans and bottles and empty cigarette packs. But there wasn't anybody there when we turned up one of the trails and left the school behind us.

The weather was still pretty cold, and the afternoons were still dark. Under the trees it was even darker. But winter was definitely on the downhill slide and if you looked hard enough you could see the first signs of spring there in the woods. I felt safe in the trees, cut off from everything. Even though I could still hear the traffic on the avenue, I could pretend that I was off somewhere in the wilderness. If I tried, I could even imagine what Long Island must have been like in the early days before the white men came. Scotty and Harrison were Indians, and I was exploring for signs of game on the trail. I guess we were careless, because when I picked up my head again, I saw that we weren't alone.

"Harrison! Scotty!" I yelled, but it was too late. Carmine Galante was in the path in front of us.

"Well, well. What do we have here?" he said. He was holding a tree branch, slicing off the bark with a big pocketknife. "Looks like you took the wrong way home today."

Harrison and Scotty stopped short. The three of us started to back away from him.

"Ain't that too bad?" a voice said from behind us. The other two WHEELS stepped out of the bushes and cut off our escape. We had walked right into a trap.

Scotty took a step toward Carmine. "Get out of the way," he ordered.

Carmine laughed and just ignored him. He was slicing long strips of bark off the stick. He looked around to be sure we were alone. "It's time," he said, "to cut you down to size, shrimp."

The others laughed at his joke.

"Get out of the way," Scotty said again, "or else-"

"Or else what? We aren't in school now. And there aren't any teachers to get in the way. We still got some unfinished business to settle. You made me look bad-"

"You were born looking bad," Scotty said and Harrison and I laughed.

"You little turd," Carmine said and made two quick cuts on the stick. "You're either braver than I thought, or else you're a lot dumber, and you don't understand how serious the situation is." The three of them closed in on us. "First we'll get rid of those jackets and then-"

I was so scared. Harrison's face was sweating and covered with hives. Scotty's fists were twitching as he got ready to fight. The three of them came in like wolves on a kill.

"It looks like your luck just ran out. Three little freaks-"

"And two *not* so little *niggers*!" Another voice said from my right. It was Duncan and Ali. Their dark shapes came out of the shadows of the trees onto the path.

My heart was beating so fast I could hear it.

The expression on Carmine's face changed. The others looked at him for some direction. "What do you *boys* want?" He flashed the blade of his knife. "This is none of your business, so why don't you *boys* get lost. Go back where you came from."

"Yeah, back to Africa," Frank LeBeau said with a smirk.

Duncan ignored the remark about Africa. "We think it *is* our business," he said easily with his Southern drawl. "We think maybe *you boys* are the ones who better get lost. Ain't that right, Ali?"

"Yeah," Ali said. He was holding a piece of bicycle chain that was hanging down at his side. He started to swing it a little. Not hard or anything, like he was just kind of playing with it, like it just happened to be there in his hand and he hadn't made up his mind what he was going to do with it. But I think Carmine had a pretty good idea what he *might* do with it.

"We wouldn't want anything to happen to our little friends here. You know?" Duncan pushed his way into the circle and took my books. I didn't realize how big he was until he was standing next to me. He was holding a piece of chain too.

"This is WHEELS business," Carmine warned, but there was a little catch in his voice. "You're sticking your noses where they don't belong, Dumont."

"You mean our flat, black, *nigger* noses?" He was eye to eye with Carmine. "That *is* what you called them, isn't it?"

Things were pretty intense for a second. I think Carmine thought about starting something, but Ali made his chain whistle in the air a couple of times, right over Lester Cooper's head and finally the WHEELS backed away.

"Come on," Duncan said. "Me and Ali want to walk you home." He led me past Carmine and the five of us walked away real slow. Ali brought up the rear. He kept casually turning around to be sure they weren't following us, swinging that chain the whole time, and smiling.

"I thought we were dead," Harrison said when we were out of the woods. His face was one giant red blotch.

"Thank you," I said to them. I put out my hands for my books, but Duncan just kept carrying them.

"Duncan and me want to thank *you*," Ali said. "When we moved up here we took a lot of stuff from those crackers. But no more. We saw you stand up to them, so we decide it's time to stand up to them too."

"This afternoon we overheard the WHEELS making plans about you," Duncan said. "So me and Ali thought we'd stick around after school and maybe lend you a hand if you needed us to even the sides a little."

"We're glad you did," Harrison said.

Scotty had been very quiet the whole time. "You know," he said finally hesitatingly, "I'm sorry," he started, "for all those times the WHEELS called you names. And for the things I said too." He offered his hand to them and they shook.

"That's okay," Duncan said. "Forget it. People like us, we got to stick together."

It was really neat the way it all happened. It was like the FREAKs had become catalysts, you know, those things we learned about in science that cause change. Only it was the FREAKs who were stirring up change at Vanderville.

# Chapter Fourteen
# "March Marches In"

The Ninth Grade Dance was a big tradition at Vanderville. It was a combination semi-formal and costume party. Kids who wanted to dress, pulled out all the stops. Some of the boys rented tuxedos and the girls wore gowns. Other kids who wanted to dress up, came in costume. A few kids even hired limousines for the night.

The dance was the first in a series of events celebrating the coming of spring, the end of the school year, and the Ninth Grade's passing up to the high school. It was the beginning of the "social season" in Vanderville. That included a float parade and a car caravan through town, the Ninth Grade trip, and it concluded with graduation. In all, it was a period of about three months. So even though it was barely March, everybody could almost feel summer already, and the hot days soon to be spent at Jones Beach. So the whole school was excited, even the teachers.

This year the theme was "March Marches In," and the dance was officially called the "Ninth Grade March In Dance."

A week before the big night the gym was sealed off. The windows on all of the doors leading into the gym were covered over with paper, so nobody could see the decorations inside until the night of the big dance. All of the biggest jocks were on guard by the doors with orders to keep everybody who didn't have a special "Student Council Decorating Pass" out of the gym. The whole time the decorating was going on, Phys Ed classes were held outside, if the weather was warm enough, or in the smaller old Girls' Gym.

All week there was a whole lot of activity in and around the gym while everybody on the Decorating Committee, including Mr. Fagan, was busy making carnations out of toilet paper. That was to spell out "Vanderville Trojans" and "Ninth Grade March In Dance" all across the gym. The school did something like that every year, and there was always a big picture of the gym in the center pages of the yearbook.

Doreen McFeeley had offered me a decorating pass and asked if I wanted to help make carnations. I told her I was too busy with schoolwork, which wasn't exactly true. But since I wasn't going to the dance anyway, I didn't care about decorating the gym. Except that wasn't exactly true either. I really would have liked to see what it looked like.

"So," Scotty said when I told him how I felt, "just do it. If it really means so much to you, why don't you help decorate and go to the dance? Half of the kids go without dates."

"No," I said flatly, "it doesn't mean *that* much. Besides, you heard what Mr. Fagan said about being excluded from the dance."

"He said *I* couldn't go, and Carmine. He didn't say anything about you and Harrison."

"Well," I said, "you know the three of us are a team. All for one and one for all. I wouldn't think of going without you. It just wouldn't be any fun. I was just a little curious about how everything is going to look, that's all. I've never been to a semi-formal costume dance before."

"Me neither," said Harrison.

Then that little light bulb lit up over Scotty's head again. His face got that peculiar look like it did whenever he was planning some mischief. "Then you're going to see it! We're *all* going to see it! We're going to *crash* the Ninth Grade Dance!" He folded his arms and nodded his head as though it had all been decided.

"Sometimes I don't understand you, Scotty." Harrison had that worried look on his face. "We just get out of one scrape and you come up with another thing to give me ulcers. *Everybody* will be there. The teachers, and Mr. Fagan. If we go to the dance, and he sees us, we'll be suspended for sure, or expelled. Or worse. That's just inviting disaster."

"I told Hildy she'd see the gym, and she will. I didn't say anything about actually going to *their* stupid dance. We're going to hold our *own* dance. It's just a coincidence that *both* dances are going to be on the *same* night."

"Are you delirious?" Harrison pushed his glasses up from his nose and scratched his head.

"No, I'm serious. We'll hold our dance here in The Pit. We can decorate it and bring our own music, and some food, and stuff to drink. While those monkeys are sweating in the gym, we'll just have our dance right here. And on the way in we can sneak a peek at the decorations. Come on. What do you say? We can do it! It'll be fun! It'll be exciting!"

It was so crazy. But Scotty seemed to have it all worked out, at least in his mind. And he was all worked up about it. I guess that's why Harrison and I said yes to him, finally. It was *so* crazy! And Scotty was right, planning it, sneaking in without getting caught, and holding a private dance right under their noses *was* fun and exciting. In fact, the FREAKs dance became the *second* most important dance at Vanderville.

So we spent the rest of the week getting The Pit ready. Harrison had an old cassette recorder that he brought from home. I got some tapes and Scotty brought in the decorations. We didn't have a lot, just some crepe paper and some balloons. And Scotty made our very own banner that he printed on an old bed sheet. He hung it on the back wall of The Pit. It said, "The FREAKs Show!"

On Friday we brought in the food. It was only a couple of bags of chips, some cookies that I had baked the night before, Ritz Crackers and Cheez Whiz, and a warm bottle of Coke. We figured that would be plenty.

I really didn't know how we were going to get into the school Friday night, but Scotty said he would find a way. The trickier part was telling my father why I was getting dressed to go out. It was a miserable, foggy night. I didn't particularly like the idea of telling him a lie, but I didn't want to go into details about the FREAKs dance. He'd make a big fuss and ask a lot of questions. So, I just told him that Scotty and Harrison were coming by to pick me up because we had to go to a special meeting at school. And that wasn't lying exactly, even if it was stretching the truth a little.

"Tonight? But it's horrible out. You can't see three feet in front of you it's so foggy. Maybe the meeting's been called off."

"No," I said, "I'm sure it isn't called off."

"If you have to go, I'll drive you."

"That's all right, Daddy. You just relax and watch the TV. You worked hard all week. We've made other arrangements. I think Harrison's mother is dropping us off." That was just a little fib.

When the doorbell rang I was ready and waiting by the door. I had my mother's ballet slippers tucked under my jacket. I don't know why I took them exactly. I guess I thought it would be kind of nice to take them to my first real dance. And it made me feel warm inside and kind of close to her having them with me.

Harrison was all wrapped up for a hurricane. His glasses were misted over. Droplets of water rolled down along the bottoms of the frames and dripped on his face. He had to use his finger like a windshield wiper. Scotty was wearing a black cape and top hat that made him look like the Phantom of the Opera. His face was done with Halloween makeup. There were dark circles around his eyes, and red around his lips, like blood.

"We brought this for you," he said. He handed me a box he was holding.

I opened it and saw that it was a flower.

"It's a wrist corsage," Harrison said. " It cost eight dollars. We both chipped in."

"It's beautiful." I slipped it on. It was the first time anybody but my father had bought me flowers. "Thank you." I kissed them both on the cheek. "I'm sorry I didn't think to get you anything."

We walked to school. It was real creepy out. Where the patches of fog touched down in places it was impossible to see your own hand in front of your face. The fog was like a pillow sitting on top of the night, muffling the sounds. There weren't many cars out, but when one did pass us, its lights left faint traces that hung in the air. In other places everything was crystal clear, and it was like you could see forever.

When we got to school we hid in the bushes by the war monument on the side lawn and watched. The entrance near the gym was all lit up, and the fog swirled in the glow of the lights. There was a parade of kids walking inside, or just standing around waiting to go in. Some were wearing suits and gowns, and some were in costume like Scotty.

"Look at that!" Harrison said. "It's Mr. Fagan!" He was wearing a pink rabbit suit and standing at the door taking tickets and welcoming the kids as they walked up. "How are we ever going to get past him?"

"We'll wait until the dance starts and then I'll find some way to get in," Scotty assured us.

So we waited. And pretty soon everybody outside went inside. Even Mr. Fagan disappeared from the door. Just a few of the latecomers ran up before the doors closed.

"Now's our chance. Come on."

Scotty led the way. He cut across the basketball courts to the entry. He managed to slip his fingers into the crack between the door and the frame and push his comb into the opening. Then he pulled and the door opened.

Even before we got inside, we could hear the beat of the music rushing out at us. It wasn't a real band or anything, just a D-J spinning records.

The lobby was empty. The gym doors, closed so long, were open wide and unguarded for the first time in a week. Inside there was crepe paper and toilet paper carnations everywhere, and streamers hanging from the baskets at each end of the floor. A mirrored ball was turning slowly in the center of the gym, sending dots of light spinning all around. Some of the kids were already dancing, but most of them were just standing around trying to look cool.

Mr. Fagan was by the D-J waiting for the music to stop. He was holding a microphone, kind of like a rabbit holding a carrot. He looked so silly. He was getting ready to give his welcoming speech and officially begin the festivities.

We crept past the gym and along the wall, trying to stay in the shadows until we finally came to the corridor that led to The Pit.

"Oh, oh," I said. "It's sealed up." A portable iron gate had been stretched from wall to wall, blocking the corridor.

"What do we do now?" Harrison asked. He kept looking back toward the gym, as though he expected the hand of doom to fall on his shoulder at any second.

"Piece of cake," Scotty said and snapped his fingers. "No *problemo*." He pressed himself flat against the wall and made himself as small as possible. In a few seconds he wriggled through the gate and smiled at us from the other side. "You next, Harrison." He held the gate as far as he could from the wall.

"I don't know if I can." Harrison stuck his head through and then his shoulder. Mr. Fagan's voice boomed out of the gym and down the dark corridor.

"Let out all of your air," Scotty said.

Finally Harrison managed to squeeze through. His face was red, and there was a little scratch on his cheek from a screw that was sticking out of the gate. "Piece of cake."

Then it was my turn. I tried real hard to fit through. Both of them were pushing the gate, but it was no use. I just couldn't seem to bend my leg enough.

"Give me your hands, Hildy," Scotty said, "and I'll pull you through." He pulled with all his strength, but I was stuck tight. Half of me was in and half of me was out. "One more time."

At the same time Harrison felt along the gate and found the iron rod that held it in the locked position. He pulled it out just as Scotty pulled me in. The gate snapped free with a loud clatter and I bounced into Scotty. We both ended up on the floor.

Harrison stood over us holding the iron rod.

"Piece of cake," I managed.

Then we groped our way along the wall in the dark until we came to The Pit.

# Chapter Fifteen
## "Back To The Pit"

"Well," Scotty said, "here we are *again*." He stood in front of the door to The Pit. "But let's do this right. Make believe it's a surprise, like the gym. Shut your eyes and don't open them until I tell you." He cleared his throat. "Boys and girls of Vanderville Junior High School," he did his best imitation of Mr. Fagan, "as principal of *your* school, it gives me great pleasure to welcome you, one and all, to our very own sideshow. In point of fact, tonight is the direct result of your collective hard work, the blood, sweat, tears and toil of Vanderville's very own *freaks*!" He pushed open the door and snapped on the lights. "Well, what do you think?"

We opened our eyes.

"It sure doesn't look like the gym," Harrison said.

"But it looks nice," I added.

"And when we turn the lights down," Scotty said, "it'll look even better." He hit the switch and everything went pitch black again.

"I can't see a thing," Harrison complained. Then he tripped down the steps and landed with a muffled thud.

"Are you all right?"

"I think so," he answered from below us, "but I don't think the soda survived."

"Don't anybody move," Scotty said. "Wait until your eyes get used to the dark."

We waited and they did adjust. The outside moonlight peeked in and out of the fog and filtered through the skylight in the center of the roof. It softened everything into shadows and light. Soon I could see everything in The Pit and I could almost read the banner that was draped along the back wall. Harrison was sitting at the bottom of the steps, rubbing his elbow. The plastic soda bottle had a hole punched in its side. The warm soda was fizzing out in a stream that spread in a darker circle on the floor.

"Don't worry about the soda," Scotty said. "I can sneak back to the gym and get some more." He helped Harrison up. "Now let's light some of these."

He produced a bunch of candles from his jacket under his cape. He lit one. The flare of the match was like fireworks in the dark, and the light of the single candle made exaggerated shadows that moved when Scotty walked. He dripped some wax on the card table and set the candle in it. Then we lit the others and arranged them around The Pit.

"Freaky isn't it?" Scotty was standing directly over a lit candle. The light made his darkened eye sockets black like a skull's. He grinned and his teeth showed brightly out of the shadows.

"Listen!" Harrison said. "What is that?"

The floor of The Pit was vibrating, a low and steady beat that I could feel in the pit of my stomach.

"Sounds like the music from the gym," I said.

Scotty opened the door and the music got louder. "It sure sounds like they're having a good time."

"Well, let's have some of our *own* music," I suggested. I put one of my tapes into Harrison's cassette player and the sounds of Mozart filled The Pit. "It isn't exactly the kind of stuff they're playing in the gym, but it's all I had."

"Let's eat," Harrison said. He fished around for the snacks.

"Shhhh!" Scotty warned. "I think I heard somebody!" He rushed back to the door and looked down the hall. I turned the music off.

"W-Who is it?" Harrison asked. He had a Ritz Cracker all Cheez Whizzed, but he was too scared to stuff it into his mouth.

"It must be g-g-g-ghosts!" Scotty cackled, and he howled. His voice echoed down the hall. "There isn't anybody," he said when he came back into The Pit.

"Do you really think the school does have ghosts?" I asked even though I didn't actually believe in that stuff. It kind of gave me the creeps to think about the possibilities. It also gave me a little comfort too, that the spirits of people we love might be watching over us.

"Could be," Harrison said with his mouth full. "There is an old Indian burial ground behind the ball field. If you look real hard around there you can still find paint pots and arrow heads and stuff."

"If there *are* ghosts in this school," Scotty said with a laugh, "it's more likely the poor souls who died trying to pass algebra." He looked at the snacks that were laid out on the table and the puddled soda on the floor. "How would you guys like some *real* food instead of this stuff?"

"You're not really thinking about going back to the gym?" Harrison asked.

"Sure. I can slip in while everybody's dancing, get some stuff and be back again before anybody realizes it. How about it? Want to come, Harrison?"

"Not a chance. Sneaking by the gym once was enough for me. And besides, I like Cheez Whiz and warm Coke."

"Well, don't start the party without me," Scotty said and he disappeared out the door before we could stop him.

Harrison went to look after him, but he couldn't see anything down the dark hall. He shut the door and we set up the plates and things and waited for Scotty to come back. A few minutes later we thought we heard scratching on the door.

"Scotty, stop fooling around," Harrison called, but when he opened the door the hall was empty. "I swear I hard something." He shut the door again. "Welcome to the *Twilight Zone*."

Then we did hear Scotty's voice. "Hey in there, open up! Open up quick!"

Harrison ran up the stairs again and pulled the door open. Scotty had his hands full.

"They have all kinds of stuff in there. Pretzels, olives, potato salad. And a couple of twenty-foot hero sandwiches. Well, one of them is only about nineteen feet now." He set the food down and three bottles of soda that he had stuck in his pockets. "Everybody's dancing. The kitchen was empty. I got in and out like a phantom." He passed things around.

All the excitement must have made us hungry, because nobody talked for the next few minutes while we devoured everything Scotty brought back, along with the stuff we already had. It really was like a party.

"That was great," Harrison said, finishing off the last piece of his sandwich. He sat back and stretched. "Hey, Hildy," he asked when he saw the pink slippers I had brought, "what are those?"

"Nothing. Just some old ballet shoes. They belonged to my mother. I really don't know why I brought them." Now I felt kind of silly that I had.

Harrison examined them and then Scotty took them.

"Hildy," he said, "I just had another great idea. Why don't you dance for us?"

"Dance? Me?" I could feel my face getting warm. "I couldn't. I'm not a dancer."

"You brought the slippers," Harrison said.

"And you said that dancing was your fantasy. So what better place than right here in The Pit, and what better audience than us, your best friends?"

"Come on, Hildy," Harrison prompted. "We have music, and candlelight. It's a once in a million chance."

"I can't. The only place I've ever danced is in my head, and in my room. I'm no dancer."

"And I'm no musician," Harrison said, "but that doesn't keep me from trying to play this thing." He fished into his pocket and came out with something I didn't recognize. "My mother always wanted me to learn a musical instrument. I think she meant the violin, but I picked this. It's called a 'Jew's Harp,' but my mother thinks that's anti-Semitic, so she insists that I call it a 'Jaw Harp.'" He put it between his teeth and plunked it a couple of times. He was able to make a melody by changing the shape of his mouth. "It's a lot harder than it looks. And if you're not careful you could lose a couple of teeth."

"Hildy, if you dance for us, Harrison can play his harp. And I can read you something that I wrote. What do you say?"

"Well-" I hesitated.

"If you want, I'll even read first." Scotty patted his pocket and took out a folded sheet of paper from his pants. "It's something I've been working on ever since the day I read Poe. I started writing it because of what you told me, the both of you, that instead of just being angry I could write. And that I *should* write to let other people know how I feel. It isn't finished yet. And it still needs work. And it isn't very good, but I want you to hear it. It's a poem called 'Invisible.' I even made a copy for both of you."

He handed each of us a copy and Harrison and I listened while Scotty recited the words. This is Scotty's poem just the way he read it.

## Invisible
### by Scotty Dwyer

It's a world full of giants, with their heads in the trees,

With their nose in the air, and their thoughts in the breeze.

But no one can see *me*, no one at all,

   because I'm no giant, I'm really so small.

In fact, if you look, I'm not there at all.

It's good I'm invisible, at least in a way,

   but it's hard to keep going when I'm nowhere each day.

Sometimes, in the darkness, when I need to be there,

I sneak up on my mirror and I stretch and I stare,

   but the space is so empty, and nobody's home.

So I crawl down the molding and scribble a poem,

   that tells of this dwarf kid who needs someone to know

   that he's living and breathing in a world down below.

But no one will read it, and nobody hears,

   and no one can see my invisible tears.

Some day they *will* notice, in spite of everything,

   the day when the giants proclaim the dwarf king!


"Scotty, that was great!" Harrison said when he finished. He got up and put his arm around Scotty and gave him a hug. It was really nice the way he did it, kind of natural and everything.

"Do you really like it? Do you really think it's good? Do you really think I could
be a writer like Poe?"

"Even better," Harrison said and Scotty looked so proud.

"Well," I said, "I guess it's my turn now." I went to the cassette player and picked
through the tapes until I found my favorite, *Swan Lake*. "Just remember, I *never* danced
for anybody in my life, not even my father."

I started the tape and the music began to play. Scotty handed me the ballet
slippers. He and Harrison watched me tie up the shoes. And then I danced for them.
knew how I looked whenever I tried it in front of the mirror, kind of clumsy and jerky.
knew I wasn't very good, but that didn't seem to matter. Scotty and Harrison followed my
every move, just like I was a *prima ballerina*. And that was just how I felt. My feet
moved in my mother's shoes and I *was* a ballerina.

"*Bravo*!" Harrison cheered when the music ended. He and Scotty were both on
their feet giving me a standing ovation. It was my dream come true, even if it was just for
a minute.

But before the sounds of the music faded completely, everything changed
suddenly, and the dream became a nightmare.

"Oh my God!" I barely whispered, looking past the two of them at the open door
I think I screamed and Scotty and Harrison jumped as three skeletons marched into The
Pit.

"Isn't this a cozy little scene?" a familiar voice said.

I tried to pull back from them as they advanced down the steps toward us. They
were so scary. With the white bones of the costumes reflecting the candlelight, they
looked like real skeletons. I tried to run away, but I fell.

The three of them laughed. "Get a load of the crip. She thinks she can dance and
she can't even stand up."

Harrison was backed up against the steps. Scotty was cut off from the rest of us.
The door was shut and blocked. Once again we were trapped. And it didn't look like
anybody was coming to the rescue this time.

"So, this is where you've been hiding out," Carmine Galante said. He peeled
away the skull mask and grinned. His face was even more frightening. "No wonder we

couldn't find you. It's lucky that Choo-Choo saw the three of you trying to sneak in tonight. Lucky for us, and unlucky for you. I guess you aren't as smart as you thought. This is a *very* convenient set up." He looked around The Pit and crossed over to me. I was still on the floor, unable to get up. I was shaking. He reached down and pulled the slippers off my feet.

"Leave her alone!" Scotty warned. He and Harrison both made a move toward me to protect me. "Keep your hairy paws off of her!"

"How sweet," Carmine mocked. "And that was a sweet little poem you read. We heard you. It brought a tear to my eyes too. Right fellas? Just before I puked!" They laughed. Carmine held the slippers in his hands and crushed them. "Hey, crip, what else do you do for these two wimps besides dance? Do you play house with them?" He threw the slippers down and grabbed me by both arms. "This *is* a convenient set up. Maybe you'd like to play house with us. Masher, lock the door."

Harrison tried to get between us. "Don't you touch her, you *Neanderthal*!"

"Neanderthal?" He turned to face the other two, still holding me by the arms. "I don't think Jack-Off means that as a compliment. Do you, you faggot?" He let me go and whipped around real fast and hit Harrison right in the face, not a slap, but a real punch. Harrison's glasses went flying and he fell hard. He hit his head, and in a second his nose started to bleed. Harrison's leg began to twitch and he moaned, but he didn't get up.

"And now it's your turn!" Carmine made a lunge for me.

I tried to get away from him and to Harrison, but Carmine got his arm around my neck and started wrestling me to the floor. I wanted to kick him and scratch him, but he was too strong for me.

"You know," he said looking at my face, "you wouldn't be so bad looking if you weren't a crip." He made a grab for me and I heard my blouse tear.

"Cut it out, Carmine," Frank LeBeau called from the door. He had pulled off his skeleton head, and I could see by the expression on his face that he wasn't too happy about the way things were going. "Leave her alone."

All this happened very fast, the way things do when you're in an accident or something, but it all seemed in slow motion. And even in the dim light of the candles, I could see everything in vivid detail so clearly. Then Carmine was on top of me, trying to kiss me. I could see the blackheads and the pimples on his face and I could smell beer on his breath and the sourness of his perspiration.

At the same time Scotty was in action. Choo-Choo Cooper had him pinned against the wall, but Scotty slipped by him when he turned to watch what Carmine was doing to me. He grabbed for Scotty, but Scotty ducked under him and jumped on the landing. He quickly untied the rope that was attached to the skylight in the roof, and used it to swing across The Pit. He moved so fast he was a blur. And from deep inside of him came a growling sound, more like a snarl, that echoed in The Pit. It made the hairs on my neck and arms stand on end.

It distracted Carmine too. He turned to see where the sound was coming from but it was too late for him. Scotty slammed into him with such force that it sent Carmine off me and into a pile among the cartons. The impact jarred loose the candle from its wax fastening. I watched it fall free and topple to the floor, and roll against the wall. In an instant the edge of the FREAKs banner caught fire. And in another instant the flames were crawling steadily toward the cardboard cartons and the cans of duplicating fluid.

"The candle!" I called, but nobody seemed to hear me.

Scotty was on Carmine, kicking him and punching him, making that terrible noise the whole time. The other two WHEELS were rooted to their spots, like they were hypnotized, just watching the flames get higher. Harrison was still on the floor, not moving at all. I tried to reach him, but there was a flash and an explosion, like the pop of a paper bag or a small firecracker. And then The Pit was full of smoke.

I felt two hands grab for me. It was Frank LeBeau trying to pull me away from the fire. "Come on! Come on!" he was yelling. "We got to get out of here!"

But I broke free from him and felt along the floor for my mother's ballet slippers, and for Harrison. It was getting impossible to see. Then there was a bigger explosion and a blast of heat that almost made me pass out.

"Scotty! Harrison!" I managed through the smoke.

"Hildy!" It was Scotty's voice that answered me.

"Scotty, where are you?" I watched him crawl toward me out of the smoke and fire.

"Stay down, Hildy, close to the floor and follow me! Let's get out of here!" He pulled me along the floor to the door. I don't know how long it took. And then I heard the fire alarm go off somewhere in the hall.

Frank and Choo-Choo were yanking on the doorknob, but the door wouldn't budge. The lock was stuck.

"Help me! Help me! Somebody please help me!" Carmine was yelling. He was blocking the door, banging on it. He was crying and on the edge of hysteria. "I don't want to die! Please God, I don't want to die!"

"Move! Get back! Out of the way!" Frank commanded, but Carmine slumped up against the door and blanked out, kind of like a mouse does when it realizes it's going to get eaten by a snake or something.

But Scotty had other plans. He grabbed Carmine and shook him real hard. "Step away from the door! Get back!" Scotty ordered, still shaking Carmine, trying to get him to respond. "Let them open the door." The smoke was choking, and the heat was intense. Scotty grabbed the collar of Carmine's costume and yanked.

"No, no. Don't," he pleaded. "Leave me alone." He tried to fight back, swinging wildly. That was when Scotty hit him, right on the chin. It made a noise like a punch in the movies, and Carmine fell down in a pile like a puppet whose strings had been suddenly cut and sat there like a rag doll. His eyes rolled back in his head and his tongue stuck out. The blood poured out of his nose.

"Don't just stand there, help me," Scotty ordered the others. "Move him away from the door." They lifted Carmine from under each arm and rolled him out of the way.

Then we heard a moan coming from behind us, from the burning center of The Pit.

"Harrison?" Scotty said. "Where's Harrison?" He looked back into the fire. "You stay here, Hildy, and I'll get Harrison." He inched back down the steps and into the hell fire. "Hang on, Harrison. I'm coming."

There was a loud bang and the head of an ax smashed through the door. Then somebody reached a hand through and pushed it in. The rush of air caused the fire to flare, and I guess the skylight shattered. Bits of broken glass showered down from the roof like the stars were falling out of the sky. The rest was total confusion. I remember

being dragged from The Pit by somebody, and the cool, fresh air on my face. My mind
was full of firemen in smoke masks, a giant pink rabbit and glowing skeletons. They all
moved around and around in a Halloween nightmare, until I passed out.

# Chapter Sixteen
## "Last Good-Byes"

In the hospital nobody wanted to tell me anything. I tried asking questions, but the nurses just smiled, or ignored me completely. Later it was my father's face that told me. He was in the hospital room holding my mother's ballet slippers. He was looking at me in a way he never had before, or at least in a way that I had never seen.

"What's going on, Daddy?" I struggled against the tubes and stuff that were stuck into me.

"Thank God you're safe," he said. He had been crying. His eyes were red. "I thought I lost you too."

"And what about the others?" It was all starting to come back to me, the dance, The Pit, the fire. "Tell me, Daddy, are they all right?" I tried to raise myself out of the bed.

He reached down and gently squeezed my hand.

"Harrison?" I asked through my own tears. "Something's happened to Harrison!"

"Harrison's all right," he assured me. "He was full of smoke, like you were. He has a nasty bump on his head and a mild concussion. But he's fine now. I saw his parents in the waiting room. And the other three–" His voice trailed off. "They told the police everything that happened."

"And Scotty? How's Scotty? What about Scotty?"

My father didn't answer me, but the look in his eyes was enough.

"No!" I said. "Not Scotty! Not him!" I started to cry and I couldn't stop. All I could picture was brave Scotty going back into The Pit.

"I'm sorry, Hildy. They got to him too late."

"But he was safe! He saved *me*! He saved us all! He went back for Harrison! It isn't fair! Life just isn't fair!" I was screaming, and I guess I got pretty hysterical.

A doctor and a nurse came running in when they heard me. I tried to fight them off, but they held me down and gave me a needle that put me right out.

Harrison came to visit me the next day.

"You look terrible," I said, and he did. His head was bandaged and his glasses were taped. And he had two black eyes. His face was cut.

"How are *you* feeling?" he asked.

"All right, I guess. What about your head?"

"Oh, they took some x-rays but they didn't find *anything* inside," he joked and tried to make me laugh. And then he added, "I think I'll live." But when he realized what he had said he lowered his head and started to cry. After a while he said, "This is for you." He had a little present that he held out for me. "My parents bought this for me in the gift shop, but I thought you might like it. It's caramels. I only ate a couple."

"Thank you." I accepted the box, but I didn't feel much like eating anything.

We sat quiet for a while. Harrison was on the end of the bed playing with the buttons that made it go up and down. Neither of us wanted to talk about what happened, but we had to.

"You know about poor Scotty?" he started. "I guess it was pretty awful for him. I don't remember much." He bit his lower lip to keep it from quivering. "The firemen reached him before he was burned, but it was the smoke that got him. They couldn't revive him. They tried for three hours. My parents told me." He blew his nose in a tissue that he took from the box on the tray. "Hildy, it should have been *me* that died in The Pit! It's *my* fault that Scotty's dead. If he hadn't come back for me-"

"It's *not* your fault, Harrison. Scotty did what any best friend would do. If it had been the other way around you'd have done the same thing."

"I'm not so sure. I don't know what I would have done, Hildy. I'm not brave the way Scotty is." He stopped and thought about what he had just said. "I mean, the way he *was*. I'm not a hero, I'm a wimp. Just like everybody says I am."

"Stop it, Harrison. You're no wimp. The first time I saw you, you stood up to the WHEELS. And when Carmine came after me, that was you who tried to protect me."

We were both crying.

"Your friends know you're no wimp. Scotty knew it. We're a team, remember? One for all, and all for one. Sometimes people die, and there isn't anything you can do about it. You can't go through life blaming yourself and feeling guilty about everything. You just have to remember the special people that come along in your life, and count yourself lucky for knowing them. Sometimes, Harrison, bad things happen to good people." I guess I was saying it as much for myself as I was for Harrison, and I wasn't just talking about Scotty. I was thinking about my mother too. "Scotty did what he did because you were his best friend, and because he loved you. And I love you too, Harrison."

I think that made him feel better. I know it helped me get through the next couple of days. Scotty saved Harrison's life, and he saved mine too. That was what we had to remember. Only I couldn't picture that he was gone, forever. Any minute I half expected to see him come bursting through the door, or to call me on the phone. It sure was hard thinking of Scotty in the past tense.

Harrison's mother and father came for him the next day when he was released after a few more tests. My father picked me up in the afternoon. He had made arrangements to take the week off from work so he could be with me. It was a quiet ride home from the hospital.

Harrison and I had missed Scotty's wake, but we went to the funeral. It was a *big* event. All the seats at St. Philomena's Church were filled. It was a day off from school, and everybody was there, all the teachers and Mr. Fagan. In a way it was kind of hypocritical. All those people who hardly knew Scotty when he was alive, all those kids who teased him and called him names, and made fun of him, they were all crying and shaking their heads and acting like Scotty had been their dearest friend.

In the church Harrison and I sat near Scotty's family, his mother and father, his two brothers and his sister. They seemed to be taking it pretty well, until the priest spoke. He talked about how God sometimes worked in mysterious ways, how God sent hardships to some people and called others back home prematurely. The priest ended with a quote from the Bible. "Greater love hath no man than to give his life for his friend." That's when Scotty's mother collapsed and his brothers had to hold her up. Harrison and I were holding on to each other.

Then, when the mass was over, Mr. Fagan delivered a ten-minute eulogy. He told everybody how Scotty was a spark plug in Vanderville, a credit to his school, his family and his community. He said how everyone at Vanderville was going to be "just a little bit smaller" now that Scotty was gone, and how they were all going to miss his happy smiling face in the halls. He ended up by leading everybody in the school song, while the cheerleaders, who were in costume, shook their pompoms. I looked at Harrison and he shook his head. I think Scotty would have laughed. It was *so* silly.

Finally everyone filed past Scotty's coffin on the way out of the church. It looked so little standing alone in the center aisle.

A couple of days later Harrison and I went to the cemetery to say our last good byes. There were flowers on the grave and the fresh dirt was piled up high in front of the headstone. We had brought a copy of Scotty's poem. Harrison read it out loud. Then we tried to tape it on the stone, but the tape wouldn't stick because everything was so wet from the first April rain.

Harrison was holding my arm. "Good-bye, old friend," he said, "and thank you." He put Scotty's poem on top of the headstone and held it down with a rock. "I hope you get a chance to show this to Edgar Allan Poe."

"Good-bye, Scotty," I whispered.

Both of us were holding on to each other and crying pretty much.

* * *

Well, I guess that's pretty much the whole story. Like I said, I'm still trying to sort things out, but life goes on. I've been talking to a psychiatrist once a week, about Scotty, and my mother, and some other stuff that has been bothering me. My father thought it might help. He's been going too. He also thought a change of scenery would do us both some good, so Daddy quit his job on Long Island and we moved again, to Arizona this time. It's funny how coincidence works in life. The city we moved to is called Scottsdale. I didn't even finish out the year in Vanderville, and in September I'll be the new girl again starting in a new high school.

Harrison and I have written a couple of letters, and we talk on the telephone now and then. He says that things have pretty much returned to normal at Vanderville, although the WHEELS broke up. And Carmine's parents sent him to a military school.

Of course I still have my FREAKs jacket. I'll keep it always as a reminder of Harrison – and Scotty.

# The End